All About Charming Alice

by

J. Arlene Culiner

Blake's Folly Romance

All About Charming Alice

Cover Art by *Jennifer Greeff*

The Wild Rose Press, Inc.
PO Box 708
Adams Basin, NY 14410-0708
Visit us at www.thewildrosepress.com

Publishing History
First Edition, 2023
Trade Paperback ISBN 978-1-5092-4853-7
Digital ISBN 978-1-5092-4854-4
Previously Published 2018

Blake's Folly Romance
Published in the United States of America

In no time at all they were leaving the restaurant. How had the evening slipped by so quickly? Disappointment smothered Alice's happiness as they stood under a million shivering stars.

Jace was watching her. He'd probably seen the disappointment. He noticed pretty well everything.

"What's wrong now?" he asked.

"Wrong?"

"Your face is as easy to read as the instructions on a jar of instant coffee."

"How unflattering. I've always wanted to be a woman of mystery."

"You are. You hide a lot. But not your emotions."

"Phooey." Resigned, she shrugged. He wouldn't let her off the hook; a man with determination was rough going. "I was enjoying myself so much. Now it's over. I feel like Cinderella, climbing into the pumpkin coach, heading back to my wicked stepmother and ugly stepsisters."

His laughter rang out, a warm sound she was getting used to. "The dogs wouldn't like hearing that."

Was he laughing at her? She didn't care.

"Besides, who said the evening was over?"

"It isn't?" Alice blinked.

"Cinderella gets a reprieve." Jace's voice was strangely gritty. "I'm not letting you escape so easily. Who knows when I'll get another chance to whisk you through the thorn barriers of your forbidding castle?"

Praise for J. Arlene Culiner

"Loved the story, the characters, the setting…a great choice for those of us in the 'older' population who would like to sit down and enjoy a mature romance with mature characters."

~ Chattykat

"A great read with a fun, quirky, and different setting. You won't be able to put it down until you know what happens next."

~ Min

"Gosh, I enjoyed this book immensely. The humor during Jace's courtship of Alice and her self-doubts often had me laughing out loud."

~ D. Larios

"Culiner's writing is magnificent. Strong and deliberate dialogue doesn't let us go until the perfect ending."

~ Sheila Clapkin, author

"Simply charming! Loved the desert setting and the unexpected profession of Alice. The dogs also added to the overall warmth of this story."

~ Romance Lover

Dedication

Many thanks to my delightful editor,
Eilidh MacKenzie, and thank you to everyone at
The Wild Rose Press.

Alice opened the door and found that it led into a small passage, not much larger than a rat-hole: she knelt down and looked along the passage into the loveliest garden you ever saw.

Lewis Carroll
Alice's Adventures in Wonderland, 1865

Chapter One

The Yellow House

The back seat of Jace's car looked like it needed a shave. "Can't you dogs keep your hair on?"

The shaggy black animal wagged its tail, a look of simple adoration in its eyes. Jace sighed. His day was going all wrong. He didn't like dogs, didn't like dog hair, and didn't like being late. Yet here he was, late for his appointment and busy driving a shedding mutt around a ramshackle agglomeration no one could call a village or a community. A semi-ghost town? Yes, that was the right word for this jumble of shacks, run-down frame houses, beat-up trailers, and car wrecks strewn along weed-choked lanes.

Hard to imagine that a hundred years ago Blake's Folly had been a wild town, a Gomorrah, a name that had brought terror into the hearts of honest men and women but also a refuge in a harsh, hostile wasteland. Times had changed, all right. Nowadays there was nothing appealing, nothing welcoming, and nothing threatening about the place. It was definitely a has-been.

"Jeez!" Jace muttered. "Why would anyone choose to live in a mess like this?" As if in response to the question, which was, of course, merely rhetorical, the dog shifted forward and licked his cheek.

Jace jerked away, threw the creature a sour look in

the rearview mirror. "The last thing I need is a dog with all the answers."

The dog was large—very large. Its bulbous head seemed to sway on a sagging neck. Its legs were long, knotted, and spindly, and its ribs wanted to punch through a dull, ratty-looking coat. Yet, ugly though it was, the damn thing had a strange appeal.

But was that a reason to talk to it? Jace had never had a conversation with an animal in his life—folks who did were either nuts or absolute fools. "And there's no way I'm sliding into one of those categories!" he stated with definite emphasis. The animal's tail thumped a mocking denial on the seat.

Jace groaned. It was all the fault of the dry Nevada air. "Doing strange things to my brain. I need the city, with big city dirt, pollution, and noise. Spend a few more hours in the desert with this beast, I'll find myself explaining the theory of relativity to it." He turned again. The amount of dog hair on the back seat had now reached disaster proportions. He had to get rid of this animal and fast.

Suddenly, the rutted track came to an abrupt end. Jace slammed his foot down on the brake, and the car skidded to a dusty stop. Now what? Ahead of him, the countryside stretched out in beige desert monotony: endless, lifeless, treeless. The man at the gas station had told him to take this dog to the last house in town: a yellow mansion. One belonging to a woman called Alice Treemont—how was that for a moniker? Certainly seemed appropriate for someone who lived in the desert and took in stray dogs. He could picture her, too, hair dyed ruby red, cigarette hanging out of a corner of her mouth, her body molded by leopard-print latex. Or else a mean-lipped witch, one who hated every male on Earth.

Jace stared at the structure on his right. High, ancient, rickety, made out of wood, it looked nothing like a mansion and more like the typical haunted house found in amusement parks. Could this be what he was looking for? Impossible. He peered out at the landscape: left, right, behind, ahead. Nothing else. Just this.

"And the locals call that yellow?" Sure, it must have been yellow once…around a hundred years ago. Back then it might have been regal.

Opening the car door, he stepped out onto the soft, brown dust that, to his annoyance, instantly covered the fine Italian leather of his boot. Hell on Earth, that's what this part of the world was. He was really looking forward to getting back to Chicago with its art galleries, concerts, and theater performances and to meeting up with the good-looking, sophisticated women he knew. But for the next month or so, he was stuck out here, doing research. It was his own fault: sometimes he had crazy ideas.

****

"Seems to me every female needs a male around the house," Pa Handy declared in his usual know-it-all tone of voice.

Know-it-alls drove Alice to distraction. She might be a deceptively fragile-looking woman, but she was rarely cowed. Now she scowled belligerently at the pot-bellied man in front of her. "Seems to me we have differing opinions on that subject." Her voice was dangerously low.

Not in the least bit threatened, Pa stared right back with complacency. "Seems to me one of us is sure to be wrong. Take this broken-down water heater, for example. Now if—"

"Male or no male, appliances wear out," Alice interrupted, hoping to bring this utterly worn-out subject to a definite end, although trying to stop Pa from giving unwanted advice was harder than blocking a flash flood. Yes, he meant well. But he was nosy and interfering like everyone else here in Blake's Folly.

Dolefully, Pa scrutinized the scramble of nuts, bolts, and rusty screws curled into the palm of one gnarled hand. "Sure they do, but it's mighty nice having someone around to put things back together again. I bet Brad Mace would've fixed this water heater in no time. If you'd let him in through your front door, that is. Got all sorts of odds and ends on that ranch of his, Brad does."

"I have no intention of asking Brad for anything," Alice countered tersely. Ask Brad for help? Why, he'd interpret the request as a mating call. Read deep, dark, hidden meaning into it. Seduction. Invitation. As far as Alice could judge, Brad had been alone in the backcountry for far too long.

"Seems a pity to me, Brad living way out there," Pa pursued, as if reading her thoughts. "You stuck here, on the far edge of town, in a house that's falling apart. Both of you on your own. Both of you lonely and single…"

"This house is in fine shape. All it needs is a fresh coat of paint and a few repairs. Besides, I'm not lonely. And if I were desperate for a partner, Brad Mace is definitely not the right one for me."

"How do you know if you don't make an effort to know him better? He's a good man, Brad." Pa nodded in stubborn confirmation of his own opinion. "Nice modern place he's got, too. All he needs is a good woman to take care of it for him."

Was she really going to let herself be dragged into this conversation? Obviously she was, if only to put all thoughts of a sizzling romance with Brad Mace out of Pa's mind once and for all. If only to click off the matchmaker's gleam in his little half-moon eyes.

"Pa, I hope with all my heart that Brad finds the good woman he needs, but that woman will never be me. I don't want to take care of anyone's house, for one. And two, I didn't come back to Blake's Folly to get married. I came here to be alone and to be in a place where I can find a reasonable number of snakes. I write about snakes, photograph, and protect them. As you well know, Pa, that's my profession. I'm a herpetologist. But like most people, Brad Mace happens to hate snakes. Brad Mace kills snakes. Brad Mace is too damn stubborn and ignorant to accept that snakes play a very necessary role in our ecological system."

She noted how her voice had risen. It always did when talk came around to this particular subject. Snakes: the most unloved creatures on Earth, and it was her duty to save them all. To educate others so they appreciated them as much as she did.

Pa frowned. "Snakes. Not a fit thing for a woman to be interested in, you ask me."

"Okay, Pa. Subject closed."

So what if she sometimes thought it would be nice to share life, hopes, and ideas with someone she loved and who loved her? There was no way she'd admit that to Pa Handy or anyone else. What would be the point? What was the chance of finding a man who shared her interests out here? No chance. That's the way life was. She'd taken the risk when she'd decided to return to Blake's Folly, flee her disastrous marriage to a successful Hollywood film director and inveterate womanizer, abandon her career as an actress, step out of a lifestyle that had made her miserable for years.

She'd come to live in this dilapidated Nevada home built by her great-great-great-grandfather in 1864 and had found the peace she'd craved. For twelve years, she'd been trudging over the desert's barren beauty with the stray dogs she rescued, and she'd never felt healthier or stronger. But that didn't stop her from, sometimes, dreaming about love. On the other hand, she refused to give up her principles and all the things she believed in just so she wouldn't be alone anymore. That's exactly what a friendship or a conversation with Brad Mace would have meant.

"Pa? Can you fix the water heater or not?"

Pa rubbed his unshaven jaw with the back of his left hand, waved the heavy wrench in his right. "Dunno. Gotta fuss around with it a bit before I decide. Tricky things, these real old-fashioned heaters."

Well, it didn't sound that hopeless, did it? There was a chance he could do something. Buying a new heater would cost her good money, and in Blake's Folly, money was a commodity scarcer than rainfall.

Although not quite as scarce as the right man to love.

Chapter Two

Killer

Impossible to miss the hum of an engine on the bumpy trail leading to the house—a car coming up this way was something rare indeed. Alice left the kitchen, went into the parlor, and peeked out the front window. A Land Rover skidded to a stop and out stepped a man, tall, strong looking, with curling reddish-brown hair. He jerked open the car's back door and called out, "End of the line, Killer!"

Killer? Something large and black seemed to unfold, stretch, and then, on unsteady legs, unenthusiastically pad out onto the dust of the yard.

The man turned, stared up at the house. His expression told her all she needed to know: he wasn't exactly sneering, but he looked incredulous.

Okay, the house no longer had any discernible style—not Western, not Victorian, not anything—and some parts did look as though they would fall to bits in the next few minutes. But there was beauty in the old place too: large bay windows stared out at a bleakly beautiful landscape; an ancient rattan settee on the broad, somewhat sagging veranda invited you to sit, relax, slow down, take the time to look out at the dusty, bare hills, the endless sky. Think about life, wonder what all the hustle and noise was about.

Alice shoved the silly thoughts out of her mind. Sure, that was the way she'd felt when she'd come back, but why would a man like that one notice such things? Look at him. No longer young—perhaps close to her age—with tight muscular thighs outlined by obviously expensive jeans and broad shoulders stretching out a fine brown suede jacket. He was—yes, she had to admit it— wonderful-looking. He also looked like a typical well-off, well-toned city man with things to do, places to go. Definitely not the sort to waste admiration on the scenery in a one-flea community.

"Come on, boy," he said and strode up the rough path leading to the wooden porch. Killer trailed behind him with meek resignation.

In the second before the man knocked on the door, his eyes caught the sign pinned to the wooden framing: ROOM TO RENT

His lips twitched with amusement...of course. He was the sort of person who would think living out here was a great joke. She knew why he'd appeared on her doorstep, too. Wasn't it obvious? He'd brought his dog and was about to abandon it. Yes, she'd seen it before, heard all the stupid and selfish excuses people gave when they wanted to get rid of a loyal pet. Her house was usually crammed full of these canine rejects—until she managed to wheedle folks into adopting some of them.

He knocked again.

Okay, he wasn't going away. Alice left the parlor and pulled open a front door whose hinges groaned excruciatingly, like that on a fairground's haunted house. She quailed inwardly at the comparison.

Looking up, she met a pair of amused and steady green eyes. "Yes?" she said, keeping her voice icy, uninterested.

The man stayed silent for a long minute, taking her in with an uncompromising and curious gaze, noting her faded, shapeless print dress that suggested anything but seduction and her pale hair plaited into two thick, old-fashioned braids. Not the sort of woman he was used to, she was sure of that.

"*You're* Ms. Alice Treemont?" he asked finally.

Alice nodded, almost imperceptibly. She couldn't miss the surprise. Surprise? What had he been expecting? A nice, elderly grandmother type who spent endless lonely evenings knitting socks? A scrawny, suspicious old witch who loved animals and hated human intruders? A hard-boiled, desert woman, cigarette dangling from a corner of her mouth, hair dyed tomato-red?

"I was told by a man at the gas station that you take in stray dogs."

She nodded again, giving no smile, offering no politeness, meeting his evaluating gaze evenly, examining him in the same way he had observed her, up and down, from head to toe. But not with the same interest most women probably showed when meeting him. No, she'd keep her distance.

Because, immediately, she knew he was a charmer, the sort of male women reacted to. His features were uneven, stark, and creased enough to avoid being pretty, and his body was lean and muscular—the type women adore. And they'd smile, try to captivate him… Well, those weren't reactions he'd get from her. Certainly not. She wasn't a woman who'd appeal to him anyway. He'd go for those who were sophisticated, elegantly fashionable.

So why did his eyes linger on her lips and leave them with a burning feeling that was as strong as a caress? She smothered the sensation, rejected the spell of his aura.

"And since you take in dogs, I've brought you Killer."

Alice crossed her arms across her chest, shifted slightly, and slowly, oh-so-insolently, leaned back against the doorframe. "Just like that?" Her voice was smooth, freezer-chilly.

"Like what?"

"Like that, you abandon your dog?"

"He's not my dog."

"He's your cat?" Alice sneered, mean enough to bite.

The man shifted impatiently. "Look, I'll start at the beginning. That way we'll get to the end as efficiently as possible. Because I have to hit the road. I have people waiting for me."

Yes, she'd already worked out that he was a man with no time, that the loud, busy world was the one calling out to him. She'd met his type before—many, many times. These days she knew enough to keep people like him far away from her life. She didn't bother hiding her sarcasm. "Of course. I understand. You're in a hurry. You want to dump your animal—an animal that loves you—as quickly as possible and get on with your life. That's what you're saying, isn't it?"

"No. That's not what I'm saying. Wrong. All wrong."

"Look at the way he's staring at you!"

The man looked down at Killer. It was true. The dog was watching him with a soft, liquid gaze. With love…pure love.

"Calm down, Ms. Treemont. Not you, not anyone is going to put words into my mouth. Fact is, I found this dog standing in the middle of the highway about eight miles from here. It took me half an hour to convince him to climb into my car, another hour trying to find out if he belongs to anyone. As far as I can tell, he doesn't. He isn't wearing a collar. Until I fed him what was going to be my lunch and gave him my last drop of water, he was starving. He's skinny as hell, so I reckon he's been on the road for some time. And," he concluded defiantly, "I was told you take in strays. So here I am. And here's Killer."

"He obviously adores you! And you're going to abandon him."

"This is exactly the sort of situation I don't need," the man grumbled. "I thought I'd do my duty, hand the animal to someone competent. And now I'm being accused of lying!" His breath puffed out in irritation, and his fingers twitched.

Irritated enough to grab her shoulders and shake her until she believed his story? The instant the thought crossed her mind, it astounded her. Not because she felt afraid. But because, strangely enough, her shoulders almost ached for his touch. What was going on? *I'm going mad. Finally. The desert and isolation have taken their toll.*

"So how do you know his name is Killer? If he's a stray, as you claim. If you found him."

"I don't know. I thought there might be certain names people give to dogs—names like Rover, Rex, Spot. Killer was more fun as a temporary handle." He waved his hands, a gesture of hopeless amusement. Strong hands, tanned hands. Virile, somehow, like the man himself.

Alice forced her eyes back to his face. Saw he was smiling. Faintly. Almost as if he'd caught her thoughts. She flushed, hoped desperately he didn't know why.

"Now do you think I'm telling the truth?" he asked more softly.

"I'm trying to." But she did believe him. Something in his green gaze told her he wasn't the sort of man who lied. Or was she being silly, allowing herself to be dazzled by that obvious charm of his? By the resolute jaw, the straightforward tone of voice, and his tight, warm-looking skin. Once again, she shoved thoughts of his aura and physique out of her mind.

The smile was still sitting on his lips. "Actually, I'm not a dog person. I've never owned an animal in my life. My mother even refused to let me have a guinea pig when I was a kid."

Alice's own lips twitched in an answering smile. She didn't want to sympathize—he was too dangerous, too sexy—but here she was, about to melt completely. To hide her confusion, she crouched down, began stroking the dog's head. "He doesn't look much like a killer." Her voice also sounded a lot softer than she wanted it to. Way too soft.

And that wasn't all. For some reason, she wanted this man to stay. Stay right here where she was, right here on this veranda. Out here in the bleak light. Of course, the very thought was ridiculous. He wanted to get away as quickly as possible, hadn't he said that? There wasn't anything in his behavior that hinted, even vaguely, at anything else.

"As soft as butter."

Alice looked up, blinked. Soft as butter? She was?

No, of course not! He was talking about the dog. His smile had broadened wonderfully, become a grin, the kind of natural grin really nice people seem to manage. One that makes resistance hightail it out of the picture, pronto.

She struggled against the grin's allure. "Obviously Killer adores you." She forced more frost into her tone.

"Then it's a case of one-sided love at first sight. I never saw this creature before this morning." He raised his arm, jabbed a forefinger at the Rover parked in the dusty lane. "See those license plates? Illinois, right? Why would I drive all the way out here from Chicago, thousands of miles, to Nevada, to dump my dog?"

She had no answer to that. Instead, she addressed the dog, speaking to it softly. "Hi there, Killer."

"He's a pretty good-looking dog," the man conceded. "Or at least, he will be when he fattens up a little."

"So why don't you keep him?"

"Keep him? Keep a dog? Yeah, right. That's all I need. Believe me, I have no space for animals." His lip curled. "No space for all the dog hair, either."

She stood up again. "How would you know? You've never tried. It's a lot more fun walking a hairy dog than a guinea pig."

"Look, Ms. Treemont, I probably sound like a hardhearted, self-centered egomaniac to you, but I did care enough to stop for the dog, then bring him here so he'll be taken care of. We simply have no future together." He stopped, lifted one shoulder in what could have been a gesture of embarrassment. "What'll happen to Killer now?"

"Nothing is going to happen to him. He seems

13

perfectly docile. He'll stay here with me unless I find a good home for him."

"I see." The man's eyes roved over the ramshackle building, took in the peeling paint, fraying wood, and sagging steps, all the things a steady income could repair. "Look, I've never brought a dog to a…to a refuge before. Can I give you some money for his upkeep?"

Money? Alice always needed money. Or fewer animals.

"Don't bother." It was pride speaking now. She hated anyone guessing how tight finances were.

"If you're sure…" He sounded doubtful.

"I'm sure," she said. Turned her attention to the dog again.

"Well…I'd better get going then."

"Fine." She didn't meet his eyes. Waited. But he didn't move. Why was he hesitating? Why did it suddenly seem less important to be on time for his appointment? As if he were searching around for a reason to tarry.

That was what she'd like. Too much. Bewitching eyes and a gentle sensual mouth that broke up the harsh planes of the strong jaw. Something primitive and elemental stirred deep inside her, as if every teeny nerve was supremely aware of his masculinity. Perhaps she could keep him here—for a little while. Invite him in for a cup of coffee…

No. That was something she couldn't do. Not if she knew what was good for her. She pushed back the feelings. She knew what this was: raw sexual attraction. In this case, one-sided. Lust for a passing stranger? Ridiculous.

He was saying something now…what? She forced

herself to concentrate.

"Thanks for taking Killer in, Ms. Treemont."

She nodded but didn't trust herself to speak.

The porch steps creaked wearily as he went down them. Unable to resist, she watched him cross the yard, open the door of his Land Rover. Climb inside. He started the engine and, after a brief wave, slowly drove back down the track toward the main road.

Alice continued to stand on the porch as the car disappeared in a hurricane of dust. Gone.

"You'd better say good riddance," she said to Killer, who was also observing the departure. "No decent human being would abandon a friend like that!"

But Killer didn't seem to be the least bit distressed now that the man was gone. He simply looked up at her and wagged his tail. He was perfectly happy.

"I must say, Killer, you seem to have a real talent for love at first sight." Not like her. Love at first sight? *No way*.

****

"Good-looking man you were talking to out there." Pa Handy was lounging in the dark hallway, the wrench still clutched in his hand, his half-moon eyes shimmering slyly.

Alice closed the front door behind her. "Didn't notice," she said, as briefly as possible and with a shrug to indicate that such things were far beyond her sphere of interest. That she had no time for tight, tugging reactions, for thoughts about how she'd really wanted to behave with that man. Thank goodness he was gone and would never come this way again. She didn't need trouble lounging on her front porch, and she didn't have any place for upheaval in her well-planned, well-ordered life.

"You didn't notice that he was good-looking, eh?" Pa's grin oozed from ear to ear. "Well, I was looking out the window, and he sure noticed you."

Alice gaped at Pa for a split second while her mind whizzed with indignant fury. "You were what?"

"Looking out the window. Watching you both. Eavesdropping." Pa wasn't the least flustered. In fact, he looked mighty pleased with himself.

"As if spying on people is the most natural thing in the world. You should be ashamed." Alice tried to sound as chastising as she could, although, in reality, she adored Pa.

Unperturbed, Pa guffawed. "I'm an old geezer. Don't have enough time left in my life for shame. Yep, he liked you, all right. And that's one good-looking dog." He evaluated Killer. "Skinny as hell, though." He looked up, his eyes twinkling. "About as skinny as you are, woman. Both of you need to get some meat on your bones."

Alice stared icily at the elderly man. "And you need to get some meat off your bones."

Pa didn't take offense. He never did. "Oh, I don't know about that. Seems to me a man my age has earned the right to a big belly. Besides…" He was looking as sly as the boa constrictor that had devoured an elephant whole. "I'm not aiming to please anyone."

"Neither am I!" It was more an explosion than anything else.

"It wouldn't hurt if you did. That's what everyone says."

Alice rolled her eyes in exasperation. Oh, for heaven's sake! Did every single citizen in Blake's Folly spend their time gossiping about her, suggesting she needed a man in her bed?

And what about Mr. Green Eyes? Mr. Oh-So-Sure-Of-Himself. Did he also think she was a frustrated, lonely woman ready to snatch at the first male that came her way? Was that why he had looked her over in that appraising way? How humiliating. Well, she'd managed to get rid of him quickly enough, that was for sure. Now all she had to do was get rid of nosy, interfering Pa.

"Let's get back to the water heater."

"Sure, I can fix it. But not today, Alice. Nor tomorrow, neither." He held out a grayish coil. "I need to order a new one of these little thingamajigs, and heaven knows when that'll get here. The world forgets folk exist in these parts when it comes to deliveries."

"Well, that's all the more reason to get going and order the thingamajig. I hate heating up pans of water on the stove in order to have a bath. This is the twenty-first century, even if it's the first section of it."

But Pa Handy wasn't to be fobbed off easily; Ma Handy would have his head on a plate if he didn't bring home a morsel of juicy gossip. "Yep, a good-looking man, he was. When's he coming back to pick up his dog?"

"He's not," Alice snapped. "He dumped the dog off. Claimed it wasn't his."

"I see," said Pa slowly. "Don't you believe him?"

Alice let out a hiss of warning. "I don't know, and I don't care. Go home, Pa."

"Doesn't look like the kind of nice man who'd do that."

"Oh really!" Her voice dripped sarcasm. "And what does a dog-dumper look like? Do they have horns and long reticulated tails? Or do they look like you and me?"

"Nope. You won't convince me. He had a nice, kind face. As I said, a good-looking man. Too bad he didn't stick around. Well, no matter."

"You know what, Pa?" said Alice, determined to end the discussion—such as it was. "I'll bet Ma is sitting in her kitchen at this very moment with a long list of things you have to fix in your house. Things you never seem to get around to doing, or so she tells me."

A faintly nervous shadow crossed Pa's face. Ma Handy was a terror. Almost everyone in the world was afraid of her tongue—especially Pa. Under her homey, welcoming exterior, Ma Handy was a foul-tempered Napoleon with two sore feet, shingles, and an ulcer.

"Okay, okay. I'm going." With a devilish wink, Pa sidled in the direction of the door. "I'll be in touch."

"You do that."

As if the residents here in Blake's Folly could do anything other than keep in touch. Blake's Folly: population of fifty-three and growing smaller every year. All you had to do was scratch your neck in a dark room, curtains drawn, windows closed, at three in the morning, and for a week, the other fifty-two residents would be asking if mosquitoes were bad out your way.

She didn't dare breathe until she heard the front door shut and the wooden steps creak as Pa made his wending way home.

Of course, all of Blake's Folly would know about the stranger and his dog by now. If Doug Farley at the gas station had given him directions to her house, then Lainey Farley would have been on the phone to Jane Grimes two seconds later. And Jane would have told Tony, and Tony would have mentioned it to Mick

Fletcher. Any minute now, Pa would be telling Ma how good-looking that stranger had been and how he'd looked at her—Alice.

"Killer," she said, looking down at the dog sitting expectantly at her feet. "You don't know what you're getting yourself into, coming to a place like this."

Killer wagged his tail happily in answer.

"Of course, it's not as if you had a choice." Dismayed, she stopped. If the other residents of Blake's Folly could see her now, deep in conversation with this dog, then they'd surely think she was odd. They probably wouldn't be very far from the truth, either. Especially if they knew where her thoughts really wanted to go—in the direction of the man she had just met, had talked to for no more than ten minutes. A man for whom she had felt nothing less than pure desire.

Desire for a total stranger? For a man whose name she didn't know? A man she'd never, ever see again? Or would she? His face: there was something vaguely familiar about it, although she was more than certain she hadn't seen him before. If she had, she wouldn't have forgotten him.

Hooking one hip on a long wooden credenza, Alice looked out the large kitchen window. A sudden breeze caught desert dust in a gentle whirl, set the branches of wild snagtail and sticky snakeweed quivering. It almost looked as if they were shaking with laughter.

Chapter Three

Room and Board

He was back.

Somehow, Alice had known he would be: hadn't her female intuition been humming, warning her he was out here in the flatland? Now there was no missing the sound of that dusty Land Rover as it rolled up the track. She waited. The car door slammed. Then...silence. She waited some more. Nothing.

Fighting to keep her face stiff and emotionless, she pulled open the ever-grousing front door.

Here he was, looking as wonderful as she remembered, sitting on the rattan settee on her veranda as if that was where he belonged. His long muscular legs in their jeans were stretched out in front of him. A lock of reddish hair faintly threaded with silver curled over his forehead, almost inviting her fingers to touch. The cool, steady green eyes watched her with amusement.

"Yes?" It came out frostily, thank goodness. The very last thing she wanted was for him to know the effect his presence was having on her. Again. And how quickly her heart was beating.

He didn't seem to mind the frostiness one bit, not any more than he had during their first meeting. Instead, in that easy, smooth way of his, he simply crossed one ankle over the other and grinned! What did he have to grin about, this arrogant, overconfident, smug person?

Hell, this was her property; she didn't have to tolerate uninvited people! "Listen, this is private—"

"It's about the room," he drawled, effectively cutting off her protestation.

"The room? What room?" What in heaven's name was he talking about?

"The room." His grin widened as his eyes shifted over to the card pinned to the woodwork. "Room to rent, that sign says."

Alice's heart sank. Of course. Her brain wasn't functioning! But when she'd thought of renting out one of her rooms in order to make ends meet, she hadn't—not for one single second—imagined some charismatic man passing this way. She couldn't let him into her house.

"There is no room to rent. I forgot to take the sign down. I'll go and do it now. Goodbye, mister…"

"Jace is the name. Jace Constant. Easy to remember, as far as names go."

Better to forget if she knew what was good for her. Not that she could. She'd heard the name before, all right. Many people had. Jace Constant was the investigative journalist who'd won prizes for his stories before changing careers some years ago and becoming a best-selling novelist. That's why he'd looked familiar: she'd seen his face on the back covers of his books. So he was famous—although that wasn't the reason her heart was thumping wildly now. All she wanted to do was run, block out the green eyes, the sexy torso…and stop reacting like a besotted fifteen-year-old!

"And I came to check up on Killer, of course."

"Finally missing the dog you abandoned?" The

words popped out before she could stop them. She forced her mouth into a sardonic little smile.

"He's not my dog. You don't believe me?" It wasn't a question, not really. His voice was calm, assured. "Look at it this way. Why would I come back if I'd actually abandoned him? I'd have to be downright stupid."

Suddenly he rose to his feet and, in that languid way of his, crossed to the doorway where she stood. She was a tallish woman, but he towered over her. Casually, stretching out one arm, he rested his hand on the doorframe, a hair's breadth above her head. He was close, so close. His body was supple, strong and—yes, she had to admit it—warm, fragrant. The heat of him reached her over the few inches separating them, and she ached to curve into it. Aura? This man was a flesh-and-blood heat wave.

The strange, tingling excitation was flowing through her again like thick port wine. She lowered her eyes, refusing to meet his gaze, although she knew he was, once again, examining her minutely.

"And I want to take the room."

"Look, you don't need my room," she said, desperation too evident in her tone. "There's a perfectly reasonable motel the other side of the Winterback Mine, out in the direction of Logan. Actually, it's far better equipped to take in tourists than anything you'll find here in Blake's Folly."

"I know. Rider Motel. Air conditioning, cable TV, and right across from the Dew Drop Inn." His smile was wry. "That's exactly where I've been staying for the last three nights. And over and over again during those three nights, I remembered Blake's Folly and the Room to

Rent sign on your wall. And the more I thought about it, the more appealing it got. There's nothing worse than an impersonal motel room when you have to stay in an area for a while." He paused, let his eyes wander over the faded wooden framing, over the settee on the veranda. "Right here, it feels more like home."

That wasn't it, she knew. That wasn't even part of the truth. He was back because something hot and wonderful shimmered between them. Did she fascinate him as much as he did her? Possibly. Although she hadn't done anything to encourage him, not once. It would have been hard to find someone less friendly than she'd been.

Yet, there was something about him that touched her, something that had nothing to do with raw desire. Was it the warmth in his eyes? A quirk to his lips that promised humor and understanding? Or was it plain magic, the magic that happens when the right female meets the right male? Whatever it was, she'd been unsuccessful in putting him out of her head for days.

She knew she was softening.

He must have sensed that too, and he pushed his point further. "Everyone, or almost everyone, needs the feeling there's home somewhere. I'm sure you understand that."

She nodded slowly, reluctance fighting with sympathy. "What are you doing in the area?" And immediately felt the flush crossing her cheeks. She didn't want to be interested in him. She wanted to blot him out. She'd opened her mouth, intending to refuse him, but the question had popped out instead. And that had opened the door to conversation. He'd realized it too, and she could almost feel his body relax with relief.

"I'm working on a book on the Old West and how history has influenced modern development, so I'll be poking around the area for a while."

Alice couldn't help smiling. "Blake's Folly's a great place for history. Luke Warner's pig gave birth to fifteen piglets once. That was back in '32, I think."

His eyes held hers. "Nineteen thirty-three. The fifth of August. A hot month for hard work like that." He gave a short laugh. "Nothing important gets past us serious researchers."

From somewhere deep inside the house, there was a loud thump followed by a wild scraping of claws. Seconds later, a huge black dog thrust past Alice and threw itself against Jace, almost knocking him backward.

"Killer! Down!"

Killer wriggled like an eel, danced a doggie jig on the veranda floor, and still managed to stare up at Jace with supplication. He was ecstatic.

Jace bent down and gingerly patted Killer's head, then looked back up at Alice with slight embarrassment. "Normally I never pat dogs. I never understood why anyone would want to." He observed Killer again. "There's pure adoration in his eyes. It gets to me, somehow."

Killer nestled in closer, his long, seedy-looking tail wagging wildly, and Jace patted him again, this time with more tenderness. Alice's defiance melted away. She loved animals—any animal: dogs, cats, rabbits. Snakes. And this man was touching her too much. Far too much.

She had to bring her defenses back into play. "That isn't the way a dog normally reacts when he meets a total stranger."

Jace met her last semblance of hostility with his

limpid green gaze. "I'm not a total stranger. I fed him my packed lunch the other day, remember?" He looked down at Killer, grinned ruefully. "I don't know why I stopped for him. Anyway, we've been through all this already. And as I said, I'm here about the room."

She hesitated—for a fraction of a second—but he must have heard it. And that meant he'd know she'd tell him a lie. Did it matter? "There was a room, but I've already rented it out."

So. That should settle it. Now he'd have to turn around, leave, go somewhere else. Find another room in some other town. And she'd never have to see him again, never have to run the risk of feeling too much for someone. Someone unsuitable. Someone who would always be unattainable. Someone who would churn up her life, ruin the tranquility she had worked so hard to create. But when a faint desert breeze tickled a stray lock of his rusty silver-threaded hair, she ached to reach out, caress.

"Couldn't help overhearing." A gruff, over-hearty voice sliced into the silence. Both Alice and Jace jumped. Pa Handy, rubbing his hands against his rather grimy overalls, rumbled out of the house. "Here to rent the room, are you? Well, that's a good thing, isn't it, Alice? You'd almost given up hope! Now you'll have spare cash to feed all these mongrels of yours."

"Pa!"

Pa turned to Jace with a wickedly delighted grin. "Lucky thing for you, sir, I got the hot water boiler going again. The thingamajig got in from Reno this morning on the bus. Well, I guess I'll be on my way now. Give me a shout if there's another problem, Alice. Be seeing you." He ambled down the front steps and over the dusty yard, whistling a searingly painful tune in an utterly contented way.

Alice didn't dare look at Jace. "If I threw a rock at Pa Handy's back, I wouldn't have much to lose, would I?"

Jace was laughing, at her, at the whole situation. She was furious. Then the fury vanished, was followed by her own irrepressible chuckle.

"Room and board?" Jace asked before she could catch her breath.

Trying to regain some dignity, she scrabbled around for a few more excuses. She couldn't let him into her domain just like that. "Staying here won't interest you—certainly the meals won't. I'm a vegetarian." She hoped that would conjure up a picture of over-boiled carrots, tasteless, mushy peas, and gluey cauliflower. "No three-inch steaks at my house."

"Sounds fine."

She could tell he was forcing himself to sound enthusiastic. "You look like a carnivore to me, not a vegetarian." *A cannibal, a woman-eater.*

"I don't know much about vegetarian cuisine," he said, with more enthusiasm than he was probably feeling. "But I'm willing to try anything."

Now she really was defeated. She knew it. She knew he knew it.

"Do I get to come in now?"

"There are millions of dogs and tons of dog hair."

"And?"

"Other things that might be a shock to your system. As a frustrated guinea pig owner, I mean."

Their eyes locked, and she saw absolutely no mockery. Instead, there was a probing intensity, a certain tension that bespoke returned interest, appreciation, and warmth. Much warmth. Much appreciation.

"What other things?" he teased. "Ghosts? Ghouls?"

"Nothing so comfortable. Snakes. Particularly rattlers."

"Snakes? Fine."

Fine, he'd said? *We'll see*. He didn't believe her. Thought she was drumming up a few more excuses. But he'd discover the truth soon enough.

Squaring her shoulders, she turned and led the way into the dark interior of the house.

He followed her down the narrow corridor, his eyes burning into her back, taking in her narrow hips and skinny legs. The tension was almost unbearable; the whole situation was unbearable. This couldn't be happening. How could she have let him into her refuge like this?

"Here's where your meals will be served." She swung open the door at the end of the corridor. The kitchen was vast—it had once, a long time ago, been the domain of cooks and servants—and the walls had a yellowish hue only time could bring. Filling every bit of space was a chaotic assortment of ancient wood-burning stoves, heavy wooden tables, rustic chairs, old glass bottles, antique cupboards, green plants. And everything was illuminated by the stark desert light streaming through the wooden frame windows.

Jace whistled with surprise. "You never begin to know a person until you see the inside of their home. I certainly didn't expect anything like this out in the desert. It looks great."

"Thank you." Grateful warmth filled her heart. He, a dyed-in-the-wool urbanite, was able to see the beauty in the old house. Incredible!

"It's like stepping into a museum!"

"For one very good reason. My ancestors built this place, and every generation added new appliances and furniture without throwing anything out. Maybe they hoped the walls would expand."

"And you keep it the same way."

She sighed. "Apparently, I've inherited the pack-rat gene. How could I get rid of anything? I love every single stick of furniture, every crock. Unfortunately, some of the finest things disappeared years ago because the house was left empty after my grandparents died. Pillagers came in and helped themselves."

"A shame."

"Yes, it is. Come, I'll show you your room."

A broad wooden staircase twisted up to a high-ceilinged second floor. Alice climbed ahead of him. Then stopped at one door. "Is this okay?" Why was she sounding so unsure? If he didn't like the room, then he wouldn't stay, and she'd have no worries.

Jace stepped through the doorway and took in the uneven floor of wide wooden planks waxed to a mirror-like shine, the authentic rag rugs, the large four-poster bed with its heavy patchwork quilt, and the faded flower-print paper on the walls. On an ancient wooden dresser, a graceful blue vase gleamed, and a hint of lavender danced on the air. "Incredible," he murmured. Then, crossing the room, he examined a framed watercolor hanging on one wall. "Gorgeous work. Who is—or was—the artist?"

"My great-grandfather, Alexander Treemont," Alice said proudly. "He was quite well known in his time."

His eyes came back to hers, stayed there. "I was

hoping I'd find something different from an impersonal motel room, but I wasn't prepared for this."

"I suppose not…"

"It's out of date, so far from reality. It's what decorators fight to achieve but can't. This is the real thing." He watched her, his expression intense, before adding, "Naturally beautiful."

He'd win top marks for flattery, probably always did. That was his style, wasn't it? She could burst the bubble easily enough. "If you really think this is beautiful, what does your home in Chicago look like?"

He laughed. "Touché. You're right. It's nothing like this. My condo in Chicago is in the center of the city. It's filled with modern furniture, and there's contemporary art on the walls."

"So…for you, this will be a quaint bit of slumming."

His smile vanished. "No. That's unfair. Being able to stay here is not slumming. This house is something else altogether."

It was. She knew it was.

The smile slipped back again. "But that's something we can talk about this evening. Over a glass of wine."

Never! Not as long as she could prevent it. She stepped out into the corridor. "The bathroom's down the hall." Her tone was impersonal, that of an efficient landlady. "Perhaps you didn't think there was one."

"The outside of this building doesn't give you the faintest hint of what's inside. Besides, we're in the desert and—"

She didn't let him finish. "This is Nevada, USA, Mr. Constant. Not the surface of the moon."

"Jace, please. Not Mr. Constant. Jace. Jace and Alice, okay?"

No. That was not okay. First names indicated intimacy. Opened the door to vulnerability. Her body responded all too readily to him; all she wanted was to step in closer, feel his warmth. Touch him, his cheek, the tightness of his chest. "I'll let you get settled in. I'll leave a key for you in the lock on the front door. Don't forget to take it with you when you go out." Getting away as quickly as she could.

"What time is dinner?"

The question stopped her flight. Dinner! She'd forgotten about that. "You're sure it's room and board you want?"

He nodded, no doubt imagining cozy get-togethers in the yellow kitchen.

"What time is convenient for you?" She would show him exactly what their relationship was going to be. She hadn't wanted his presence here. He'd practically forced his way in. As for thoughts of intimacy, he'd better forget them.

"I'll be meeting up with a few local historians and geologists in the area or spending time out at the Winterback Mine, but I should get back here at around six every evening."

Alice hesitated, feeling as though she should add something. But what? Then turned away, headed quickly down the stairs, rushed away from turmoil and toward safety.

****

If she hoped to find refuge in Rose Badger's secondhand clothes shop, Alice was sadly mistaken. The shop was a mad jumble of hats, shoes, evening clothes, silks, and vintage dresses, all displayed in an insouciant disorder and housed in what had been the town's newspaper office a century and a half ago. Normally Alice loved coming here, making herself comfortable in the faded plush armchair and listening to stories of Rose's latest male conquests. But not today. Her life had changed, her territory had been invaded. This evening, she'd have to face Jace Constant again. What an impossible situation!

"I hear you've got a lodger."

Alice groaned. "Out of the frying pan and into the fire!" Having Jace Constant in her house as a guest—for the few days before she managed to get rid of him—was going to be a hell of a lot more difficult than she'd imagined. "Rose." Alice made certain that her voice expressed infinite fatigue and forced patience. "I've had a lodger for about an hour and a half. How did word get around so fast?"

Rose Badger opened her large blue eyes even wider. "What else is there to talk about in Blake's Folly? The last piece of gossip anyone heard around here was that Tom Nifty's car ran out of gas on the highway near Tonopah, and that was over two years ago."

"You've got a short memory. Didn't Lucy Hawkins overcook a chicken dinner last May?"

"What does he look like? Lainey Farley told Jane Grimes that she saw him when he stopped at the gas station the other day—and, according to Lainey, he's gorgeous." Rose glanced at her own reflection in the broad mirror behind the counter of Second Hand Rose and smiled.

Alice felt a stab of jealousy, then pulled herself up short. She was being stupid. Rose was the kind of woman who would interest a man like Jace Constant. Her blonde curls framed a delicate oval face. Her lips were naturally rosy and full. She was tiny, curvaceous, and a lot of fun. She was also an inveterate flirt.

"Didn't notice," said Alice sourly, crossing her fingers behind her back as she lied. The harder she tried to forget Jace Constant, the more she thought about him. Those eyes that seemed to penetrate deep inside her. The smiling mouth that suggested lazy kisses. She could picture the smooth muscles under his shirt, too.

Rose looked at her curiously. "I'll bet you didn't, either. You're a hopeless case."

"He's a lodger, Rose. Not a lover. Get that? Never bite the hand that feeds you."

"That doesn't sound right, coming from you. How many times have you been bitten by those stray dogs of yours, but that's never stopped you taking in new ones and loving them all." Her eyes sparkled mischievously. "Come on, Alice. Life is for fun."

"I have fun, and I have my own way of doing it," Alice answered primly.

"Yeah, right. Talking to dogs, defending the rights of snakes, and spending every available moment wandering around in the desert alone. Great."

"I love doing those things. Besides, they sound better to me than chewing up and spitting out all the available males west of the Atlantic Ocean."

Rose's nose wrinkled in the most adorable way. "I have fun, too. That happens to be my way of doing it. To tell the truth, I have a sneaking suspicion that the males I chew up and spit out enjoy themselves as much as I do."

"I wouldn't be so certain of that."

"Don't change the subject, Alice. We're talking about your lodger. Go on. Describe what he looks like."

Alice almost hissed with exasperation. "What do you want to hear? I can't describe people!"

"Tall?"

"You aren't going to give up, are you?" It was strange. For some reason, Alice didn't feel like gossiping about Jace. It seemed undignified, somehow, but there was no way Rose would let her off the hook. "Okay, okay. Tall."

"Hair color? Eyes?"

"Wonderful green eyes. Reddish-brown curly hair with a gorgeous touch of silver. Broad shoulders and the sexiest mouth I've seen in ages. Long fingers. Really good hands."

"I see," said Rose, staring at her friend with too evident interest.

"Fine. Now can we drop the subject?" Alice stood abruptly and walked over to a clothes rack. "This looks like a new delivery. Come to mention it, I need a winter coat. Mine's falling to pieces."

Smiling knowingly, Rose refused the bait. "My dear friend, for someone who didn't really notice what he looks like, that's a pretty detailed description. Go on. What else?"

"Nothing else. That's it. Are you satisfied?"

"Satisfied? Are you joking?" Rose was staring at her with pure, unadulterated astonishment. "How do you feel about him?"

"Me?"

"Yes. You. You sound interested."

"Well, you're wrong. All wrong," Alice answered hotly. "Actually, he's more your type. Handsome, too sure of himself, sophisticated."

"You're whetting my appetite."

33

"I'll bet I am." It was almost a relief to be on safe territory again. Almost… "Rose, I thought you were in love with Lance Potter this week."

"Lance Potter." Rose looked strangely vague. "Did I say that?"

"Unless I was mixing him up with Mike Dowd."

"Mike? You're joking." Her groan was a deeply heartfelt sound. "I'm coming to the conclusion that most men don't understand what the word romantic means. To begin with, Mike invited me to dinner. And what do you think he meant by that? The bar over near Logan, and a choice between microwaved frozen industrial pizza, or meat paste sandwiches on stale curled bread. No wine, no candles. No eye contact either. That was out of the question. So was conversation. Darling Mike was too busy watching a televised match on a huge overhead TV. I was bored out of my tiny mind."

"And that's the end of Mike Dowd."

"It certainly is. But stop trying to divert me. What's his name?"

Alice rolled her eyes heavenward. "You really don't give up, do you? Jace Constant."

Rose looked puzzled. "Sounds vaguely familiar. Tell me why."

"Because he's a writer. He's fairly famous, okay?"

"Fine. This is getting better and better. The man is gorgeous, he's famous, he's sexy. Now, Alice, tell me what's wrong with him?"

"What's that supposed to mean?"

"Why don't you want him?"

Alice gaped. "Is that a serious question?"

"Why shouldn't it be?" Rose looked all innocence.

"I can't believe this. For one, he's too good-looking."

"And?"

"Men who look that good think they're God's gift to females."

"Ridiculous! You don't know him yet. What's reason number two?"

"He's a big city man. You should see the way he winced when he looked down and saw the desert dust on his fancy leather shoes."

"So?"

Alice slapped her hands down on her thighs with exasperation. "What am I supposed to do? Go in for a quick fling? For a weekend, or a few days, or one whole month of intimacy and trust? Then give the fling a peck on the cheek and a packed lunch when he goes back to the city and his other life? Say, well, that was a nice quickie, thanks, and so long? I have my memories to keep me warm?"

"Why not?"

"Why not? Because a scenario like that is yours, not mine. I'm not like you. I'd end up caring. Falling in love. But you go ahead. Have a fling with Jace Constant."

"Right." Rose nodded. "Sounds good. When do I get to meet him?"

"Knowing you, Rose Badger, you'll drop in unexpectedly one evening." Alice's voice was surprisingly tart. She knew she was being ridiculous. Yes, Rose would most definitely be Jace's style. Rose was every man's style.

"Sure. I'll drop in—if you're so certain you don't want him."

"We're not running a cattle market here. If you're attracted to each other, go for it. I don't do quickie affairs. How about changing the subject? Have you got anything new in?"

Her curiosity temporarily satisfied, Rose was fairly easy to divert. An almost-sure way of getting her off the subject of men was to direct her onto clothes.

"Wait until I show you! A Mrs. Grady over in Whiteshaw had me take a look into some old trunks she had in her attic. Alice, you aren't going to believe your eyes. Dresses! Pure 1940s, and top quality too. Silk, bias cutting, the works. There's one in a dusty burgundy that'll take your breath away! Come, take a look. I bet it would even suit you."

"Wouldn't it just." Alice laughed. "I've always wanted to wear silk while boiling up the dog chow."

They had finally stopped talking about Jace—a man who spelled big trouble—and Alice could forget about him. For a while. Or at least she could try.

Chapter Four

Rose

"The sooner I get away from this desert, the better life will look," Jace griped as he left the dreary rutted town streets behind and began tramping over the broad stretch of oatmeal-brown nothingness. How he hated the dust that covered his soft leather boots, nudged its way into the seams of his clothing, and ground between his teeth each time the chilly wind picked up. And he loathed the dog hair clinging tenaciously to his cashmere sweaters.

As far as night life went in Blake's Folly...well, there didn't seem to be any other than turning out the lights at nine and hoping tomorrow would bring a diversion. Of course, there was also the local watering hole, the Mizpah Saloon, and if you were looking for conversations about snail racing, evil outsiders, slot machine wins or losses, dental problems, fallen arches, indigestion, poker games, and cattle ranching, that was the place to go. "Not quite my style. Not yet, anyway."

Now, if he were home in Chicago, in his ultra-modern, luxurious condominium at this moment, what would he be doing? Planning a night out with friends or sipping something pungent with the sexy luxuriant Tanya by his side? You didn't find someone like Tanya in Blake's Folly. You didn't find a man like himself here either, and the inhabitants of the place were letting him know that. Why, yesterday evening, at least seven people had "accidentally" wandered up the track that led to Alice's house and stared at him as he sat out on the veranda. Stared? God, the verb "to stare" had been invented in Blake's Folly!

Suddenly, Jace's eye caught movement at the ridge on his left. A wild animal? If he stood still, would it come closer? He'd wait and see.

He didn't have to wait long; soon enough, he saw the form was human—or, at least part of it. He even knew who it was. One person in the world would be caught in such a dreary landscape, striding forward as if she were in a lush, green valley. Alice Treemont. The shifting dark clumps around her were her many canine friends.

Well, well. All memory of Tanya's expensive perfume skittered out of his mind, taking with it every morose thought. A wave of satisfaction warmed him. Hadn't he been hoping to find Alice out here? Of course he had. Why else would he be walking in the desert? For some reason he couldn't yet fathom, Alice touched him. Not because of her looks or not solely because of them.

She was so different from the other women he knew. Her thick, old-fashioned braids, her high cheekbones, and hazel eyes—so pale, they were almost golden—fascinated him, as did her thin, elegant mouth. Perhaps her long slender figure was as lovely as he imagined it might be...or tried to imagine. Because Alice Treemont seemed determined to hide every subtle curve under the most hideous and shapeless skirts, sweaters, and print dresses that he'd ever seen—doing it in the same way she hid the real person she was behind a wall of silence.

Jace now watched as Alice came to a sudden stop on a dusty rise. Obviously she'd seen him and wanted to avoid any encounter. He saw her dilemma. There was no other track other than this faint path in the scrub. A meeting was inevitable, but over the distance separating them, her reluctance was palpable. His pleasure at seeing her turned into annoyance. Why the hell did she resist all his attempts at friendliness, at simple conversation?

Alice had consistently made a point of avoiding him ever since he'd been a boarder in her house. When he returned from work, the warm aroma of dinner greeted him as soon as he opened the door. Okay, he'd never imagined vegetarian fare could smell—and taste—so good. That was one bonus. If he needed some meat between his teeth, there was always lunchtime at the diner near the Winterback Mine. But the problem of getting to know Alice wasn't so easily solved; until now, she'd managed, consistently, to thwart him. The long wooden table in the kitchen was always set for one person. And the conversation—such as it was—had been the same every evening.

"Aren't you going to join me, Alice?"

"I've already eaten." Her voice had all the warmth of winter in the tundra.

"That's no reason."

Her eyes always avoided his. "I have things to do, Mr. Constant."

"Jace."

"Jace," she'd repeat faintly before vanishing into another part of the house.

"Thrown to the dogs again," Jace always said to the several warm, sleeping bodies stretched out in various corners.

So the meals, albeit delicious, were also lonely: fresh, homemade bread, warming bean and vegetable stews flavored with exotic spices. Where had she learned to cook like that? Surely not in the Nevada desert. Jace had a million other questions on the tip of his tongue. All he needed was the chance to ask them. Except, dawdle in the kitchen though he might, Alice never reappeared in the evenings. And breakfasts were as solitary—and as delicious—as dinner.

"Wonderful coffee, Alice."

"Freshly ground." She wasn't going to say more than she had to. He had forced her hand in renting the room, and she wouldn't let him forget it. If only she'd been a run-of-the-mill landlady. But she wasn't. She was Alice: lanky, sometimes awkward, infinitely intriguing, and downright, in her own original way, sexy.

Go slowly, Jace, my boy. Easier said than done. Patience had never been his strong point, especially when it came to getting to know women, and at the moment, his healthy male pride was taking a terrible blow.

Now, catching her out here in the desert would make her escape more difficult. She couldn't avoid talking to him or letting him accompany her back to the house. She was trapped: no way she could retreat. He felt his mouth stretching into a welcoming grin. Yes, this evening he'd get through to her. He'd come back early, so there was no way she could claim she'd already eaten. And that bottle of fine wine waiting on the Rover's back seat was begging to be shared.

Of course, seeing the almost hostile look on Alice's face as she approached didn't make him feel overly optimistic. She was about to give him the cold shoulder...as usual. Fortunately, Killer's enthusiasm set the tone of the encounter. When he realized it was Jace standing there, he began whining piteously and tugging at his leash with frenzy. Killer was certainly a skinny animal, but he was a strong one, and Jace could see Alice was having a tough time holding him.

"Let him go," Jace called out to her.

In his enthusiasm, Killer was becoming hopelessly entangled in the overly long leash, and now it had wound itself around Alice's legs. Any minute now she'd come crashing to the ground.

"Jace to the rescue," he crowed with glee and jogged in her direction. It was a very minor rescue, of course, but a very pleasant one. He felt an almost irrepressible desire to nuzzle the little hollows on the inside of her knees as he untangled her. He felt considerably less content when Killer, in a tornado of dust, threw himself into his arms and covered him with excessively soggy dog kisses.

Alice snickered at his attempt to dampen the dog's ardor.

"It looks like I've been rolling on the ground," said Jace ruefully when Killer finally lost some of his intense interest.

"You do," Alice confirmed. She caught her bottom lip with her teeth in an effort not to laugh out loud. "You don't like dust, do you?" That gleam in her eyes was a malicious one. She was poking fun at him.

"What's that supposed to mean?"

"Don't think I haven't noticed the way you polish your boots every six minutes or so."

"Old habits die hard," he grumbled.

"Or don't die at all," she countered.

Things weren't exactly going the way he'd planned. This conversation certainly wasn't. It wasn't seductive in the least. Foiled again.

"It could be worse, though," Alice added. "Imagine what you'd look like if Killer had been swimming in the gully down there." She indicated a wide, dry slash on the desert floor.

"Swimming?"

"It can be terribly dangerous when the flash floods come."

"This countryside is hostile."

"Hostile?" Alice looked up at him with sincere surprise. "I can't imagine anyone thinking that!"

"Can't you?" He raised his eyebrows. "Flash floods, wind, bleakness, monotony. What would you call those?"

"Emptiness can be magnificent." She stretched her arm out in a wide gesture. "Look at it, this glorious expanse. Smell the air. There's no place as fragrant as the desert. Listen to the wind, the crackling of dried vegetation." Her voice was rich with pleasure.

Incredible how her face changed when she let down her guard. Enthusiasm made her cheeks glow, her eyes shine. Fine tendrils of hair had escaped from her thick braids and were tickling her cheeks. She brushed them back with an impatient gesture, and Jace wished he had the right to do it. And that beautiful mouth. What would it taste like when he finally got around to kissing it? Because he was certainly going to do that. Sooner or later.

"The pioneers who passed this way didn't feel so warmly about the area," he offered, preferring neutral territory to the tumultuous terrain of his thoughts.

"Probably not."

"Definitely not," he insisted. "A bleak landscape of cocoa-brown lava extrusions and purple shadows? Sunlight so intense it makes you uneasy, but no shade to hide in? No water, only shimmering blue mirages? What about the way shapes are distorted in this sort of landscape and how distances are falsified? Some travelers on the old wagon road that passed through must have gone crazy when faced with the challenge of getting the hell out of here."

Alice looked at him curiously. "What wagon road?"

He liked being able to tell her things she didn't know. "Follow me."

She hesitated, then let him lead the way back over the small rise and through a scrabble of scattered rock. Straight ahead was a faint, almost erased bit of trail.

"Here you are," Jace said with evident satisfaction. "A hundred and fifty years ago, this was one of the great roads to California. Think about the people walking, riding, and dragging their way through this with their animals. No trees anywhere, no grass, but creosote bushes, cat's claw, and mesquite. When summer temperatures rose to a hundred and ten, pools of water turned into toxic shimmering scum before vanishing, and rivers evaporated. The way to find the trail was by following the abandoned sacks of putrid bacon, the skeletons of animals, and the graves."

Alice nodded. "I know that place names on maps—ones like Endurance, or Desolation, or Last Gap—were never more than a stick in the ground where someone was buried. And, yes, you're right about some people going mad out here. I heard of one man who killed his brother because he couldn't stand the sound of his voice.

43

Another strangled his partner because he kept twirling his moustache."

Jace quirked an eyebrow. "And you call this desert magnificent?"

Alice waved a dismissive hand. "Not a pretty picture, not an easy history, I'll concede that. But nowadays, I look at the area with different eyes. I'm not crossing it to get somewhere else. I'm here, living in peace, enjoying the calm you can find in extreme places. Besides, there are sad stories in every part of the world, not just here."

"So why not enjoy yourself wherever you are?"

"Exactly."

Now she's wedged herself into a corner, Jace thought with satisfaction.

Obviously realizing she had, Alice turned to the dogs. "Edda! Tilly, Betty. Let's go."

Jace matched his stride to hers. "I suppose I'll have to spend more time out here in order to appreciate it better. It's so different from Chicago."

The soft earth silenced the sound of their footsteps. Somewhere in the air high above them, a bird trilled brightly. It was true what she'd said, Jace mused. The desert was calming, and the air had a dusty, intoxicating tang, an odor he could appreciate. He also knew something else: Alice was softening—not that she had much choice. He was a naturally friendly person; she couldn't remain defensive in the face of friendliness. Or deny the slow sizzle that seemed to vibrate between them.

"Don't you mind living in a big city with traffic and noise all the time?" Alice asked.

"Not at all. I love it. I can't imagine living anywhere

else."

"I see."

They had reached the spot where the Land Rover was parked.

"Can I drive you back? There'll probably be enough room for all the dogs." Jace tried not to think of the mountain of dog hair he'd be cleaning out. *Going soft in the head, old boy.*

"Absolutely not." Already she was moving away. "There's nothing I like more than walking in the desert." Then she stopped, turned to him, her eyes mischievous yet defiant. "I can't imagine living anywhere else."

****

Jace lounged in a chair while Alice shredded a zucchini. He was making her exceedingly nervous. It wasn't because he was sitting there. No, it was also the way he watched her. The way he occupied that chair…as if he belonged there. Which he didn't.

Look at those clothes of his. City stuff, those expensive jeans, the gorgeous leather footwear, the sweater that was obviously cashmere. All the trappings of a city man playing at country life. An actor, playing a part. Of course, she had to keep saying things like that to herself, make an effort not to sneak little glances at him. He looked mighty good—city slicker playing a part or not. *Keep your distance if you know what's good for you.*

"Have you lived here all of your life, Alice?"

"No. My family has been in Blake's Folly since the town began back in the 1860s. My ancestors built this house with money from the silver mines they owned, but by the time my mother was born, there was no more silver and no money either. She left when she was eighteen and pregnant with me. I came out here to visit

45

my grandparents during the summer school holidays."

"So where did you grow up?"

"California."

Jace was obviously waiting for more details, details she wasn't about to give him. He whistled, waited a minute or two. Then he said, "Mighty big place, California."

She looked up sharply. Was he making fun of her? Yes, he was. His mouth was twitching. He seemed to like riling her. It was a game to him, breaking down her barriers, softening her up. She'd keep on resisting too.

She concentrated on rubbing the zucchini, pushing it furiously through the grater. How long had he said he would be staying? A week? A month? She couldn't remember. Or had he set a time limit at all?

"Where in California?"

She threw him a look guaranteed to turn the most stouthearted soul into a pillar of salt. "Nosy, aren't you."

Before she knew what was happening, he had sprung out of his seat and was standing beside her. She looked down at the bowl of grated zucchini. Why was he standing so close! She tried to move away, but he arrested her movement with strong hands.

"Alice? Look at me."

His touch seared through the thin cotton of her dress. *Fool. Letting him touch you when you know exactly where it will lead. Get your desire under control.* She recoiled. And felt how reluctant he was to let her go. But her rejection had cooled him. He took a step back before grabbing the shredder and what remained of the zucchini.

"Let me do it," he said, his voice gentle.

"I'm perfectly capable—"

"I'm not saying you aren't. But you were getting so violent with this poor vegetable, you'd have scraped your knuckles raw. And this is supposed to be a vegetarian dinner."

She fought to get her nerves under control. The shock of his touch had sent live current zipping through her body and logic spiraling out of the picture. Leaning back against the counter, she tried to steady her trembling hands. Well, it was pretty clear what he was after, wasn't it? Yes, it was. Intimacy. And what if— what if she let it happen? How would it feel to lie in his arms? As good as she thought it might be?

Repressed desire propelled her into action. She had to do something...anything...move, busy herself with a plate, a glass, fork, knife, and spoon. She had to push all the hot, dark, sexy ideas out of her mind.

"What were you thinking of doing?"

Her throat was dry, her heart pounded. "What?" It came out as a croak.

He was watching her, amused curiosity spread over every feature. "I'm finished grating the zucchini. What will you do with it?"

Relief followed confusion, turned into embarrassment. Calm down, Alice, she told herself. Calm down. He can't read your mind. She took a deep, steadying breath. "I mix the zucchini with a little whole-wheat flour, eggs, salt, cumin, coriander, and black pepper. Make fritters and fry them. They taste wonderful with fresh yogurt and mint."

"I'll bet they do. Zucchini fritters." He grinned. "I'm game."

Good. This was the way to manage: keep things nice, dull, and domestic. She curled her mouth into a challenging smile. "One of those simple, homemade dishes you probably don't have time for in big city Chicago." She sounded perfectly normal now, didn't she? With conversation on this level, he'd never have the faintest idea how he affected her. And when he left, it would be goodbye forever. She wouldn't be another notch on that belt around his waist, the one her fingers itched to undo.

Very pointedly, he directed his gaze toward the long wooden table where one place had been set. "But which one of us doesn't get to eat?"

"I've already eaten."

"Nonsense." He wasn't going to let her rebuff him again. "We've both been here for an hour, and you haven't so much as nibbled."

"You are a paying guest and have the right to privacy."

"More nonsense. I'm responsible for grating the zucchini; therefore, my status has changed to coworker. Besides, I hate eating alone."

Exasperated, Alice stared at him. Was there no way of discouraging the man? Didn't he have any pride? But he looked arch, smug. He probably didn't mind eating alone, had been doing it for years. He simply wasn't used to having his invitations refused. Women would never say no to a man like Jace. Maybe this was the first time he was meeting with serious resistance; was that why he was so determined to break down barriers? Because he needed a challenge? Because success would make him feel good? So he could go back to the city a satisfied man?

"Look, Alice? I'd like to spend the evening with you. Get to know you better. Talk. I've brought a bottle of wine for the occasion."

She stared at him for a minute. "Wine?"

"French. A Buzet."

"Nice," she said.

"I'll bet not everyone in the state of Nevada knows a Buzet is a nice wine," Jace approved.

Her eyes locked with his. Time stopped. Doubt vanished.

Until a staccato knock sliced into the intensity. The dogs all barked. Alice blinked, came up for air from what seemed to be the bottom of a warm green reedy sea. Here was the real world again, rapping at the door, begging to be let in.

"Yoo-hoo! Anybody home?"

The unlocked front door whined open, snapped shut. There was the sound of light tapping footsteps. Rose Badger. Of course. It would be. With a new man on the horizon, nothing could discourage Rose. Why had it taken her so many days to show up? And why had she arrived at the wrong moment!

"Alice?" Rose called.

Alice shoved down her feeling of irritation. Or was it jealousy? Ridiculous. Hadn't it been her idea to get Rose and Jace together? If they were attracted to each other—and they certainly would be—she'd be out of the picture. Safe from Jace, from her own emotions, from the fascination she was attempting to deny, from the riotous feeling of desire she was forcing herself to quash. With Jace gone, she'd be a free agent again. Alice tried, as hard as she could, to make the thoughts comforting.

"Ah, here you are." Rose strolled into the kitchen in that naturally sexy way that was uniquely hers—you had to give it to her: when Rose made an entrance, she did it in a big way. Then she stopped and stared at Jace. Began fluttering her lashes in a perfectly false semblance of surprise. "Oh, Alice. I thought you were here alone. Am I interrupting anything?"

Alice knew her friend's acting talents far too well to be taken in. "Rose, this is my lodger, Jace Constant."

"And I'm Rose Badger, Alice's friend." She gave her most winning smile.

Alice couldn't miss the bright smile Jace gave in return, and she felt indescribably sad. And dowdy. And like an utterly useless and very flat third wheel. She and Jace had shared a delicate, deep, magic moment, Alice was sure of it. But now she felt the magic sneak sulkily out of the room to be replaced by a new piece of theater: *The Rose Badger Show*.

Now Rose would charm the socks off Jace. She was perfectly lovely, and tonight she'd fluffed up those gleaming golden curls and put on a delicious crushed-raspberry shade of lipstick.

"Oh, Alice. What on earth are you cooking? It smells absolutely heavenly." It was impossible to ignore the hint.

"I take it you haven't eaten." Alice's tone was dry, although she did her best to muffle the sarcasm.

"I haven't, as a matter of fact. I'm starving. There were so many gabby clients hanging around the shop, I didn't think I'd ever be able to close. To escape, I claimed you were expecting me here."

This wasn't the moment to mention that Rose's clients had left her with enough time to spruce herself up for this "impromptu" visit. Alice noted the tight, soft sweater that left little of Rose to the imagination. "Of course you'll join us for dinner."

"Alice and I were about to sit down together and eat." There was a little note of teasing laughter in Jace's voice.

"She's a brilliant cook," Rose gushed, apparently unaware of any tension in the room.

"After the meals I've had so far, I couldn't agree with you more." Jace's eyes were on Alice. "Where did you learn to cook like this?"

"A question of liking to experiment, I guess. I've always loved cooking." Alice smiled. "And eating."

His eyes traveled over her body. All length and bones. Stringy, she called herself. With no luxurious curves to tempt him.

"No one in the world could put on an ounce if they walked as much as Alice does," chirped Rose, who must have intercepted Jace's glance. "She must cover at least twenty miles a day with those dogs of hers."

Why didn't they talk about something else! Why couldn't they forget her existence? Alice cracked an egg on the edge of the bowl with unnecessary violence. If only Jace and Rose would stop examining her like this—as though they were observing a strange bug under a microscope. She knew her cheeks were glowing hot pink.

"Who were your clients, Rose?"

"Rich tourists. On their way to Reno." Rose launched into a description of a woman whose face had been lifted so many times "her squinty little eyes were right up on her hairline."

Jace laughed, and conversation became general. Alice listened with one resentful ear. How well the two of them were getting on, how easygoing their chat was. Having a good conversation with Rose was so simple.

She was honest, humorous about herself and her life, and utterly spontaneous. It would be nice to be like that.

Alice chopped fresh mint and parsley on a wooden cutting board. Stopped. Wait a minute. What were Rose and Jace talking about now? Mussorgsky's opera *Boris Godunov*? Russian folklore and Eastern Europe? Fossils? What did Rose Badger know about subjects like those? Alice peered at her friend, nonplussed. But this wasn't the first time she wondered if acting like a man-crazy dizzy blonde was merely camouflage. That underneath the shallow, happy-go-lucky exterior was a far deeper, secret Rose.

By the time dinner was over, real complicity seemed to have grown between Rose and Jace, but Alice was in a black mood. The two of them had forgotten she existed. Never satisfied, she chided herself. One minute you want everyone to ignore you, and the next, you're furious when they do. Still…it would have been nice if Jace had resisted—even a little—Rose's charm.

She glanced up at the ancient longcase clock ticking loudly from the opposite wall. Rose showed no sign of leaving, nor Jace of tiring. Alice felt like a chaperone. Might as well leave the two lovebirds alone.

She stood. "Don't forget to turn out the lights, Jace." Her voice sounded raggedy, sour. For heaven's sake, what difference did it make to her if his interest in her had been so short-lived? She hadn't wanted his attentions, had she? The fact that he'd let her drop so quickly showed how right she had been in her estimation of him, of the male sex in general.

"Goodness gracious," exclaimed Rose. "Look at the time."

"Time for bed," said Jace, rising.

Alice looked at him sharply, searching for innuendos, trying to intercept a knowing glance between him and Rose. There wasn't one. In fact, they were making an effort to show they were nothing more than polite new friends.

"Bye, Alice," said Rose and gave a little flutter of her hand.

"I'll lock the door after you," said Jace.

There, that would give them time alone. Look at how quickly Jace had jumped at the chance to see Rose to the door. Well…why not use all this pent-up resentment for something positive. Alice stacked the dinner dishes in the sink with grim violence. She tried not to notice how long Jace was gone, although it seemed to be hours. She was less angry with the two of them than she was with herself and her evident jealousy.

She was so lost in morose thoughts that, when Jace reappeared with a dishtowel in his hand, she jumped. He picked up a plate and began drying it.

"What do you think you're doing?"

"Drying the dishes," said Jace calmly. "If we share the job, it'll get done faster." He examined her face. "And you look exhausted."

"But you're a paying guest! You can't do chores."

"I can. All you have to do is charge me extra." He grinned.

"Look—" Alice began.

"You're dripping soapy water all over the floor."

She was. The suds slid down over her hands.

"You can't stop me from doing what I want, you know," he said, shaking his head. "I'm a pretty determined guy."

"I've noticed," she answered sourly. Turning back

to the sink, she tackled the rest of the dishes and found, despite her best intentions, that her mouth had twitched itself into a smile.

Okay. It was ridiculous to deny the pleasure his presence gave her. Standing here, side by side, sharing this simple domestic chore, it was as if they'd been doing it together for years, that's how natural it felt. She tried to calm the fluttering of her heart. He was no more than a nice polite guest.

When the last dish had finally been put away, she moved swiftly to the door. No reason on earth to prolong this intimacy a minute longer. He followed her out to the long dark corridor where a feeble lamp burned. Pausing at the foot of the stairway, she turned. "Thanks." She kept her voice cool, impersonal, dismissive, although her nerves were pulled as tight as wire strings on a violin. "Sleep well."

He was standing too close, once again. He always did, come to think of it. The warmth of his body reached her in the dim, secret shadow of the hall. She saw his eyes drop to the curve of her lips, and his need reached her. She knew how he felt. Despite herself, despite her determination to resist, the slow flame was burning in her belly too.

He raised his hand, lifted her chin with the tip of his strong finger.

With any remaining resistance, she tried to shake her head. "No," she whispered. She saw the gleam in his eyes. He would never accept "no" if he wanted something. Hadn't he said that?

But he didn't make a move.

She was the one who stepped in closer, letting her breasts caress the tightness of his chest. She was the one who sought his lips. She was the one who showed she wanted him.

In the split second before his eyes closed, she saw the heat, the pleasure, and his astonishment. He lowered his mouth to her warm, questing one, brushed her lips, once, twice. Brushed them again. Then the kiss deepened, expressed infinite desire. She soared, responded, melted. Her hips lifted, arching against him, and when he groaned softly, a thrill of triumph flooded through her.

"Alice." It was a gasp, a plea, and a declaration, all at the same time. He pulled her closer.

She also wanted more, wanted him in her bed, wanted his nakedness against hers. But was it worth it? Worth the heartbreak of being a temporary partner in a short lusty affair? Here was raw desire. But what about other emotions? What about caring? Love? Those things weren't in the picture. They hardly knew one another.

She pulled away. "Stop, please, Jace!"

His eyes gleamed, burned into hers. Hot, cold, hot, cold, they seemed to say. He was angry and excited, curious and confused.

Taking a deep breath, he also stepped back, as if needing all his strength to do that.

Tease, she chided herself bitterly.

They were both silent.

"I want you," he said finally. "And you want me."

"I need time," she whispered raggedly. Time to think, to weigh up the consequences, to reconcile herself to the lonely misery of a one-night stand or a one-month affair: a simple conquest.

"Alice Treemont," he said, his voice a caress. "Alice with braids, a haunted house, the desert, and dogs. You have a wonderful erotic power, and I want to make love with you."

"Good night…" Her voice caught.

His finger traced a line down along her cheek, down her neck, between her breasts. She shuddered, almost wavered. Then, quickly she turned, raced up the stairs. Didn't look back.

The dogs followed sleepily, dark forms padding after her.

"Lucky dogs," Jace growled.

Chapter Five

Snakes

"Just as I expected," muttered Jace when he came down to breakfast early the next morning. The kitchen was empty. No sign of the ever-elusive, mysterious Ms. Treemont. His place had been set at the table; there was hot coffee steaming in the pot by the stove. The room was cozy, warm, inviting, and the rich smell of freshly baked muffins filled the air. Exactly the way a real home should be, he mused…except this wasn't home. Not his, anyway. He was a temporary, unwelcome boarder, and Alice Treemont wasn't going to let him forget that. What did it matter in the long run? He was a city man, not some down-home rustic.

Then, for around the ten thousandth time, he remembered the kiss they'd shared, the way her body had sought his, and his defiant thoughts vanished. He sat, picked a muffin out of the basket beside his plate, broke it open, and took a bite. His eyes closed with pleasure.

"Blueberry," he declared in a very satisfied voice. If freshly baked blueberry muffins weren't absolute total bliss, they were pretty close to it as far as he was concerned. But there was one very important element missing as far as the ideal breakfast went. Filling two cups with coffee, he set off in search of Alice. He wanted her company. He wanted to see her sitting across the table from him. And he was mighty fed up with this game of aloofness she was so intent on playing.

At this very moment, he didn't care if he encroached on her territory, delved into her privacy, or stomped in where he wasn't wanted. He wanted to know every single detail about her, and he would ferret it all out. No matter what barriers she'd decided to throw his way.

"Beware, Alice Treemont," he warned as he stepped out into the dark hallway.

The house was silent, peaceful, friendly even. He peeked into one perfectly proportioned room, then another, and couldn't help being impressed. Beautiful faded wallpaper, fragrant, waxed wooden furniture, and on the walls, more of those excellent framed watercolors portraying various desert scenes. But no sign of Alice.

Until, at the end of a long corridor, he saw a light under a closed door. He knocked. There was no answer. He turned the knob.

Found himself in an office, or was it a library? Ceiling-high shelves almost sagged under the weight of books. He noted the two inviting armchairs, a high, heavily curtained window, and thank heaven for miracles, here was Alice, sitting behind a vast, old-fashioned wooden desk covered by a messy scatter of papers and photographs. Surrounding her were, naturally, the dogs. They, at least, acknowledged his presence with happiness, opening their eyes sleepily, thumping their tails on the wooden floor before returning to their dozing.

Alice was less welcoming, but Jace couldn't help noticing the pallor of her face, the circles under her eyes. Had she had as much trouble sleeping as he? He hoped so. Now she stared at him dispassionately, as if forbidding him to approach. *Too late for that, my lady. You showed your true feelings last night.*

Crossing the room, he held out one of the cups of coffee and saw her hesitate. Clearly, she was determined to refuse anything he had to offer. But he simply wasn't going to allow her to rebuff him. Not anymore. They were going to play this out like equals.

"I'm working." Her voice was no-nonsense cold. She took the coffee he handed her, cupped it in her hands.

"Yes. I see that." *Not brilliant, Jace. You can do better.*

"Your breakfast is waiting on the table."

Trying to dismiss him again. She had a real knack for making him feel foolish. "I saw that. Great muffins. Also, the kitchen's where I got this coffee, you know."

She had the grace to look embarrassed. "Yes, of course… Thank you for bringing me a cup."

"So why are you hiding from me again, Alice?"

Wordlessly, she stared at him.

"Okay. Don't bother answering. I already know why. You're hiding because of what happened last night. Right?"

She was fighting not to show any reaction, but he saw the quick nervous flicker in those strange, almost golden, eyes of hers.

"But that's not all, is it?" he continued mercilessly. He paused. Her face had gone paler, but he couldn't stop. She had to know he wouldn't let her call all the shots. "You liked what we shared. Very much." He saw her wince as color rushed into her cheeks. "And you hate yourself because of it. I make you feel something, and that's exactly what you want to avoid. Feeling. Opening the door to emotions."

Lowering her eyes, she carefully put her cup down on the desk; he couldn't miss the faint trembling of her fingers. "Stop prying," she said, finally. "Stay out of my life."

He heard the chipped ice in her voice, felt its chill reach his bones. Decided to be tough. Not heed the message. "No way."

"You have no right to intrude." The words were harsh.

Looking at things from her point of view, that was certainly true. He had no rights. This was her life, and she could live it the way she wanted. He was the intruder. So why didn't he let go? Listen to his inner voice that told him to leave the lady in peace. That there was obviously something going on here, something too complicated to untangle. That he was here for room and board, and he'd soon be home in Chicago, away from all of this. So why persist? Why run after a woman with an intimacy issue? Why think of charming her?

But he saw the way she was really looking at him. With anger, yes. And passion. Need, too. She was no chilly woman, and she couldn't keep up her show of indifference, no matter how hard she tried. To hell with his wishy-washy inner voice that counseled prudence.

He put down his cup as deliberately as she had. Walked around to her side of the desk until he was standing right beside her, towering over her. Power position.

She looked up at him. Not with fear. Not that. She was a tough woman, he knew. Anyone could sense her strength vibrating in the air around her. Then, unable to resist the call of her fine, stubborn lips, he bent down, lowered his mouth to hers.

She wanted to fight him. Or she thought she did. Her hands rose with the intention of pushing him away. But they stopped in midair, fingers fluttering in a helpless gesture of submission. And want.

If he'd ever experienced kisses that affected him like these, he couldn't remember them. Like last night, his senses spun, reeled. And her lips opened under his, met his demand. Sliding his hands down over her back, he again felt her body arching up toward him in mutual riotous desire.

This time he was the one who pulled back despite senses running amok. Her face was flushed, her eyes half-closed in pleasure. He observed her silently for a moment. Then felt his own smile. Not a smile of triumph but one of complicity. One she returned without reticence.

She was beautiful when her features softened like that.

Of course, what he really wanted to do now was pull her up into his arms, drag her up those steps to his big, soft bed. Rip off the shabby cardigan and shapeless print dress that hid her. Possess every inch of her long, slender body. Watch passion chase away the last bit of resistance. But he knew he couldn't do that. Not yet. *Cool down, Jace. Go slowly if you don't want to be thrown out on your ear. There's plenty of time in front of you.*

Then he caught sight of one photo lying on her desk. Involuntarily recoiled.

A picture of a snake, huge, curled. Thoughts of seduction and charm went spinning out of his head. "Ugh," he grunted.

Alice's brows arched, her eyes gleamed, but not

with desire. "What did you say?"

"It's horrible."

"What's horrible?" She was relentless.

"That. That…thing. That snake. It's a rattler, isn't it?"

"And a rattler—any snake—is something you hate?"

Jace moved to the other side of the desk, preferring to distance himself from the photo, from the overriding feeling of nausea that had seized his gut. "Yes. It is." He knew it was the wrong answer to give. Alice might like snakes—that wouldn't surprise him in the least. He'd probably sealed his doom, ruined his chances with her. She'd mock him for his weakness, sneer him out of her life.

But she wasn't sneering. "What do you know about reptiles?"

"Very little." Did he really want to pursue the subject? No, he didn't. Better to be flippant and get this over with. "In a high-rise condo in Chicago, reptile encounters are exceedingly rare."

She watched him with an unreadable expression, one that gave him the feeling he had to justify his reaction. Save face so Alice wouldn't write him off as a complete coward, a frail city boy. But how could he do it without delving into the past, into the most painful episode of his childhood? He couldn't.

Jace lowered himself into the armchair on the opposite side of the desk. "Okay. I'll tell you a story."

"Fine," said Alice. "I'm listening."

"It's about something I don't like remembering or talking about. You see, I have what I suppose you'd call a terrible revulsion or a phobia about snakes. Ever since my cousin Jerry was bitten by a coral snake."

"A coral snake?"

"Jerry died."

"I see." Alice nodded. "Where was this?"

"In Kentucky. My aunt and uncle had a cottage outside a small town called Weston. I used to go out there in the summer, visit Jerry." So many years had passed since then, but Jace remembered the sandy ground, scrubby conifers, the intense summer heat, and ubiquitous noise of insects. Even the rich smells—grass, hay, hot earth, pine needles—had stayed with him, imprinted on his mind.

"Go on."

"It wasn't the most exciting place on earth, but Jerry and I made it interesting. We'd go hiking, ramble around, and discover other places in the area. One day we decided to explore an abandoned farm a few miles down the road, poke around, see if there were ghosts in the place, or forgotten treasure—you know how kids are. My aunt and uncle wouldn't have let us go out that far if they'd known, but that couldn't stop us."

"How old were you both?"

"I was thirteen. Jerry was two years older. I looked up to him as an authority on everything. He was the big brother I never had. And as far as snakes went, Jerry wasn't afraid of them at all. He liked snakes, kept baby garters as pets."

"Did he know anything about coral snakes?" Alice asked.

"He did. Or he said he did. But when we found the coral snake out on a sandy patch near an old barn, Jerry said it was a scarlet snake. That a scarlet snake can look like a coral snake, but it isn't venomous. He wasn't afraid at all. He went over, cornered it against the wall so he could pick it up, but it went for him. Bit him in the leg and held on. I was terrified. Finally it let go, slithered away. Jerry said the bite hadn't hurt, but I could see he was scared, because scarlet snakes never, or rarely, bite. So we decided to head for home. Before we were halfway there, Jerry was having trouble breathing. I had to leave him by the side of the road, run for help. But it was too late." Jace stopped. A blind terror of snakes had stayed with him since. Would remain for life, he was certain of it. Even now, he had to force himself to look at the photo of the rattler. "And that thing looks huge."

Alice nodded. "Around three feet long. They can grow to five feet or more, but that's rare."

"Are there a lot of those around here?" he asked, dreading a positive answer.

"Great Basin rattlesnakes? I found this one not a hundred feet away from the house."

"You took that picture?"

"Yes, of course. You can get fairly close when the weather gets cold because they move slowly then. Besides, Great Basin rattlesnakes are timid, and they would much rather slide away to safety than strike."

"That's exactly what Jerry said about coral snakes." And he'd paid the full price for his error.

"He was right about that," Alice confirmed. "All snakes are passive. If you leave them alone, watch them from a distance, they'd never think of hurting you. The snake that bit Jerry probably panicked because it was being cornered."

"I know that," said Jace. "I know that now. Because I had to understand what happened, I forced myself to read a bit about coral snakes. Investigated." He managed a faint smile. "It was a way of living with tragedy. And I suppose it started me out on my career of investigative journalism."

"Turning a horrible experience into something positive." Alice smiled at him, an encouraging smile. She wasn't mocking him for his fear; she wasn't making him feel silly.

"How do you know all this about snakes?" Jace asked. He'd confided in her; now it was her turn to let down her guard, tell a few secrets.

"I'm a herpetologist," she said simply. "I study snakes, I photograph them, I write about them for nature magazines. I protect them."

"Do you have snakes here in the house?" Goose bumps had broken out on every inch of his skin.

"Around the house, yes. I certainly don't chase them off, if that's what you're asking."

"I see." The list of things he had to tolerate was getting longer: desert dullness, endless dust, multicolored dog hair, horrific reptiles—all that for a woman who was rarely welcoming, who would probably like to get him out of her house, out of her life.

"If this is a problem, Jace, I can understand your wanting to leave," Alice said. "I did try to warn you about snakes when you said you intended to board here, but I didn't realize it was such a big issue."

Now she'd found the best way of getting rid of him. But he knew one thing: he didn't want to go—despite the snakes. If this fragile-looking woman had no fear of them, he could make an effort, tolerate their proximity...or try to. Yes, he'd stick around. For a while. Not for forever, of course. Long enough to get to know Alice better, see what the world was like when you looked at it from her direction. To investigate another lifestyle.

"No way I'm leaving. It's not every day I meet a genuine herpetologist."

To his great surprise, her eyes warmed like golden suns. "Good. I'm getting used to having you around."

Had he heard correctly? Had she really said that? Incredible. His heart rose. Fighting to hide how pleased he was, he stood, headed for the door. Then paused, turned. "Don't bother cooking anything tonight."

He caught the sudden disappointment she was trying to hide. "Because you won't be coming home?"

Home, she'd said? Surely she hadn't noticed her slip. "Because I'm taking you out. For dinner."

Alice jumped to her feet. "No!"

"What? This is incredible. Now what have I done? Asked you to have dinner with me? Not to go roast Killer."

"I don't go out for dinner."

"Why not?"

"Because if anyone sees us, they'll all start talking. They'll link us together, and I hate, absolutely hate, being a topic of gossip. You don't know what you're up against. This is Blake's Folly, and here—"

He didn't let her finish. "Too bad. Tonight we're going out. Together. And not to the Mizpah Saloon or the Dew Drop Inn either. I'm taking you to Lucy's. I heard it's the best restaurant out in this part of the world."

"Lucy's? You can't do this, Jace!"

"Have a nice day, Alice."

"Jace?" Her voice, almost plaintive now, followed him down the corridor. "I don't have anything to wear to a place like Lucy's."

"I've got a great idea," he called back. "Go see Rose." He wondered what Alice's tall, thin figure would look like in elegant clothes, in anything but those faded, shapeless print dresses—she seemed to possess an endless collection of them. Thin? No, she wasn't thin— those long legs and long arms gave that impression. She was nicely slender. And lanky. He smiled.

It was when he was finally driving down the main road in the direction of the Winterback Mine that he remembered the warm blueberry muffins and realized how hungry he was. He'd forgotten to eat breakfast.

Chapter Six

The Dress

"Look, Alice. Look at this dress. It's the one I told you about." Rose's eyes were shining as she held out the long sleek tube of burgundy silk.

"I can't wear something like that," Alice wailed.

"Why? Why can't you?" said Rose. She was getting more and more exasperated with every passing minute. "No matter what I suggest, you quash it with a wall of negatives."

"I can't because…because… Oh, I don't know. Because it's not me!"

"Of course you don't think it's you. You've been so busy wallowing in the swamp of unadulterated frumpiness for so many years now, you can't imagine, for one minute, that you could do something else!"

"And I thought we were friends."

"We are. If I were your enemy, I'd keep you in those awful frocks you hide yourself in. I don't need competition."

"What competition?" Alice gaped at Rose. "What kind of a joke is that?"

"Alice, sweetie, stop arguing. Okay?"

"Look, Rose, I can't pay for a silk dress. Not even a secondhand one. And I bet, even secondhand, this one costs a fortune. It's pure 1940s chic."

"We haven't talked money. And I never imagined you were a wealthy woman." Rose smiled.

"You're not giving it to me!" Alice was vehement. "Because I won't accept."

"If I gave away the things in this shop, I'd die of starvation."

"You're lending it?" Her eyes searched Rose's face. Was she imagining the embarrassment?

"I'm not a lending library either," Rose answered tartly.

"Well then, tell me the price, please." Alice was almost pleading. A dress like that couldn't come cheap. It was exquisite, and she'd love to wear it, but she had such a hard time making ends meet. Why didn't Rose show more sympathy?

Jace, too, for that matter. He was impossible; he didn't have the faintest idea how things worked out here. Soon enough, everyone in the state of Nevada would be linking his name to hers, making them into a permanent couple. Then Jace would go zooming back to his fancy Chicago world, leaving her behind, and everyone would pity her as the rejected woman. The one who'd been dumped by that handsome, very famous writer who'd stuck around long enough for a quick adventure.

"Alice, try the dress on, okay? I told Jace I thought you'd look great in it."

Alice stared at her friend, open-mouthed. Then she exploded. "Jace? What does Jace have to do with this! What are you talking about!"

Rose stayed calm. "Jace and I talked about it last night…at your very own front door, by the way. He told me he wanted to take you out for dinner, bring you to a really nice place, and he wanted me to find the perfect dress for you. Okay?" She stopped, obviously noting Alice's horrified expression, and her breezy self-confidence dissipated. "I told Jace this wasn't going to be easy…"

"Oh, you did, did you?" Had everyone on the North American continent betrayed her?

"Yes, I did," snapped Rose.

"He told you I would go out with him before he asked me?"

"I guess that's the way things look. And Jace also said that if you argued about the price, I was to explain it was a present. From him. For taking in Killer."

"I never heard anything like this in my whole life!" Alice wanted to scream with rage. "What do you both think you're doing, plotting behind my back like this?"

"Plotting? Who's plotting?" Rose's voice rose, took on a high note. "Someone wants to give you a gift and that's called plotting? You're plain nuts, Alice Treemont, and I give up! This is a present, right? Jace wanted to give you a present, and you refuse to accept, like always. Okay, go out to dinner in rags, if that's what you want. Slip into something that looks about right for washing the floor." She stopped, her eyes narrowing suspiciously. "I'm willing to bet you argued with Jace about going out to dinner!"

"How do you know?" Alice felt her fury ebbing away. She'd never seen good-natured Rose angry before. I manage to ruffle everyone's fur, she thought miserably.

"How do I know? Because that's what you're like. You're always ready to give. You're the first one in this whole state who rushes in when anyone needs help, cooking for people if they get sick, or if they break an arm or a leg. Every year you help with the Get-Together, the garage sales, and you also take care of all the helpless animals in the area. But you've never learned how to take, and that's unfair. Other people like to give, too, you know. But you don't care about that. It's *your* pride that counts."

Alice was silent for a long moment. Why was everyone ganging up on her? Or perhaps they weren't? What if Rose was right and she was wrong? Why was life so confusing? Why had her own life become so complicated ever since Jace had appeared in it? She closed her eyes. Then opened them and nodded slowly. "Okay. Point taken. I guess I'm going to have to work on this." But, right now, all she wanted to do was get out of this shop.

"Hey, kid." Rose looked at her soberly. "I care about you. And maybe Jace does also."

"Jace care about me? Nonsense. You're dreaming up a love story the way you always do. Jace doesn't know me. I don't know him."

"So, when you go out to dinner with him tonight, ask questions. Tell him things."

"And I can't accept the dress."

"If you refuse, I lose a sale."

"This makes me feel like a kept woman."

"In that case, you shouldn't accept a coffee from me or dinner from Jace. And what about Pa Handy fixing your boiler for free? Does he make you feel like a kept woman, too?"

Alice's chin jutted stubbornly. "Pa said he's going to send me a bill."

"He won't. You know that as well as I do. Give up, Alice. Try the dress on. I have a wonderful pair of pointy-toed silver high heels to go with it. Accept what Jace is offering—even if it's this once. He's gorgeous, he's sexy, he's nice, and he's not trying to buy you. He wants to please you. So…be happy."

Alice felt herself relenting. "What if I look awful in it?"

"It's not the only dress in the shop, you know." Rose's voice was tinder-dry. "And, uh…one little question, okay?"

"You've got nothing to lose."

"It's about the braids. I mean, you aren't thinking of wearing your hair in braids tonight, are you? I'm not saying they don't suit you. They do. And in Blake's Folly, they're fine…" Her voice drifted off.

"I get the message." Alice tapped an impatient foot. "Since I'll be wearing a tulip-shaped dress that will make me look like a strange stick insect and heels high enough to break my neck in, I need the appropriate hairstyle."

"Message correctly received."

****

Jace went up to his room to change. The house was silent. No sign of the dogs, no sign of the unpredictable Alice. She hadn't run out on him, had she? He didn't like to think about that possibility, although he knew there was a chance of it happening: he'd thought about it all day.

He put on his blue shirt, made a face, ripped it off, and went for the gray. No, that was worse. The striped tie that had seemed so suitable in Chicago looked miserable right now. Why had he bought the thing? Finally, he settled for a white shirt and well-cut navy slacks. He felt like a tied pot roast in the tweed jacket.

Calm down, Jace. You're taking a lady out to dinner. You've done this a thousand times in your life.

So why was he feeling like a teenager on his first date? And in Blake's Folly, of all places. Anyone would think he was getting ready for the flash of Chicago High Society. But the little voice in his head pointed out, once again, that he hadn't felt this pleased to be going out with any woman in his acquaintance for quite a long time— be it in Chicago, Paris, Los Angeles, or anywhere.

He kept one ear cocked, listening intently. No sound from anywhere in the house. He felt more and more certain she was standing him up, and his sharp shard of disappointment mingled with faint anger. Enough was enough. His male pride had been taking severe blows over the last few days, and frankly, he wasn't masochistic enough to continue with the game.

Then he remembered the way Alice's lips had felt against his, the way he'd felt her body responding to his, and the wave of hurt pride receded a bit. "But you have to know when to quit," he said to himself. If she really did stand him up tonight, he was clearing out of here. Why keep fighting a losing battle?

So, where was she? He stormed out into the hallway. She'd better be somewhere in this house. He wasn't about to go out and scour the desert looking for her.

He knew where her bedroom was: at the end of the long corridor leading to the back of the house. And right now, its dark, wooden door was closed to him, to the whole world. But doors were meant to be opened, too.

He knocked. "Alice? Are you in there?"

"Yes." Her voice was hesitant, faint.

So she hadn't run away. She'd been here all the time. He let out his pent-up breath. "Alice—uh—are you ready?"

Silence.

"Alice? What are you doing in there?"

"I'm hiding, I think." A burst of laughter.

"Why are you hiding?" He was almost shouting with relief.

"Because I feel so strange in these clothes, I don't know who I am anymore. Oh…I guess I'm feeling shy."

"Look, I'm coming in." If the door was locked, he was feeling crazy enough to bash it down. It wasn't.

He took a step into the room. Stared. Stared some more.

Damn. If he hadn't known it was Alice there, he wouldn't have recognized her. Not right away, anyhow. Her shining hair was parted on one side, caught in a tiny barrette before cascading to her shoulders in a smooth sheen. She'd put on makeup, a faint touch of mascara, shadow, and a dark blush of lipstick that matched her burgundy dress.

His eyes slid over her, not missing an inch, taking in the narrow waist, her soft curves, the long legs. She looked magnificent. "Now I see why you always try to hide yourself under faded print rags. You look wonderful." The words sounded too banal for such a radical transformation.

She blushed deeply, then smiled shyly. "You're looking pretty wonderful yourself."

"Thanks." Little veins throbbed in the hollow of her neck and he needed all his willpower not to step in closer, lower his lips to the fragrant soft skin. Why the hell did everything this woman say mean so much to him?

He held out one hand. "Ready?"

"Ready." Her long fingers curled around his. "Jace, listen. About the dress…"

He raised his other hand, warning her not to

continue. "Very nice dress. Nicer with you in it."

They were both silent as they went down the stairs. Strange. It was as if, now, he also felt too shy for conversation. He fumbled while helping her into a short wide swinging jacket. He, a man of the world, was as awkward as a ten-year-old. This was really the limit.

"I'm afraid a Land Rover isn't exactly ideal for dinner with such an elegant woman," Jace offered as they crossed the dust in the direction of the car.

"Oh, I don't mind." She smiled. "Traveling in a Land Rover while wearing a silk dress seems nicely decadent."

When they were on the highway and heading west, he again sensed hesitation on her part. "Are you certain you really want to go to Lucy's tonight?" she asked.

"Why shouldn't we?"

"It's almost in Reno."

She had tensed. "Something wrong with Reno?" he asked lightly.

"Of course not." It sounded as though she were forcing herself to sound insouciant. "It's been so long since I've been anywhere outside of the Blake's Folly area, Reno seems like the big wild and woolly world."

But as the Rover licked up dusky desert miles on the mirage-teased road, one that seemed to flow like deep water, tension evaporated. And over and over again, he sensed the caress of her brief, secret glances on his profile, as delicate as butterfly wings.

And that made him feel so good, so very good. And very, very male.

Chapter Seven

The Last Chance Saloon

When they finally arrived at the restaurant, Alice had the distinct feeling she was walking around in a dream: someone else's. Or that she had time-traveled back fifteen years—a frightening thought. *Calm down. Time travel is science fiction.* She looked around her. The elegant room was dimly lit, the atmosphere, refined. On white linen tablecloths, silver cutlery and crystal glasses gleamed. Civilization.

More overwhelming was the touch of Jace's hand burning through the skin on her elbow as he led her across to their table. People turned, watched as they passed, and she quashed the desire to run, escape before disaster struck. What if someone recognized her? What if someone remembered what had happened all those years ago? What if there were journalists in here?

But as those thoughts raced through her mind, she knew she was being foolish. Who would remember her now? She had vanished from the limelight years ago; she was older now and no longer looked like the old Alice everyone had known. Hadn't newer Hollywood scandals snared the public's unhealthy interest?

Anyway, people weren't watching her. They were staring at Jace because he was famous. And gorgeous. Too gorgeous. The firm jaw, the serious line of his brow, the intelligent folds of his skin, those eyes…his lips. Yes, hard to resist staring at the man, and she'd found herself sneaking little looks as they drove here.

Their table was a discreet one. No one was near enough to overhear their conversation. Had Jace arranged that? If so, why? What if he knew more about her than he let on? He had also been a journalist once upon a time.

But why ruin her evening? Why suspect everyone of delving into her past? She'd cope with that old drama when it came up. Better to enjoy this one evening in Jace's company. Who knew when—or if—another would ever happen? And Jace was so easy to be with, to talk to…when he wasn't asking her questions. She couldn't stop her eyes from crossing the table, grabbing another look at him over the menu he was holding. His hands were tanned, strong looking, and she had to stifle the urge to reach over, touch.

What if she did? What would he think then? That she was a desperate, lonely woman dying to leap into bed with him? Yes. That's what he'd think. And would he be wrong? No. He wouldn't. She did want him. She knew that, she admitted it. Finally. And accepted it.

All last night, she'd tossed in her bed, thinking how his body would feel against hers. How she wanted to ravish him in the most wonderful way. Taste him, lick him, smell and savor every tiny inch of him.

And all the while, she would be courting disaster. Not because she could mean nothing to him; not because their relationship would be temporary. But because letting herself feel strongly for someone would pull her back to a world she had escaped, create turmoil she never again wanted to experience. Because facts, harsh facts, would eventually come between them, and everything would be ruined. The very idea made her heart ache with misery.

Jace was watching her over the dancing candlelight. "Earth to Alice."

She laughed and neatly hid the direction her thoughts had taken. "I guess I've been out of circulation for so long, I feel overwhelmed. And light-headed from this very green and rather potent cocktail you've ordered." Whatever it was. Sweet and bitter, sour, tangy, and lovely, the drink was sending coherent thought reeling. "For years now, my social life has been the Blake's Folly Annual Get-Together, a few garage sales, backyard barbecues, and other such great desert occasions."

"And before coming out to Blake's Folly, where was the social whirl then?"

His question came out lightly, but he was prying nonetheless. She didn't want to rehash her past. It was over and done with. She didn't want him knowing who she'd been, but she couldn't remain silent: that would strike him as strange, abnormal. She hesitated before answering. "Los Angeles."

"You're from L.A.? Interesting."

Interesting? She wondered why. But she corrected the misunderstanding. "I wasn't born in L.A. I lived there for a while, but I grew up in Sacramento."

He shot her a swift glance, as if trying to sum up what he imagined to be her story. "Divorced?"

The question came so unexpectedly she wasn't fast enough to skirt it. She avoided his eyes. "Divorced."

"Children?"

"No." Vaguely, she looked into the distance, as if

thinking of something else entirely. The tense moment was eased over by the arrival of a dish of skinned, roasted green peppers in olive oil and stuffed with eggplant. She looked over at Jace, determined to change the subject. "Will you also be having a vegetarian meal?"

"I'm not that easy to convert." He chuckled. "I was vaguely thinking of ordering roast lamb for my main course. Are you offended?"

"I should be." She nodded, pretending to be hurt.

"I'm willing to reconsider, though."

"Really? You probably asked me out to dinner so you could finally eat some poor animal. Vegetarian fare is getting you down."

"No," Jace said simply. "I love the way you cook. I love the food I've eaten at your house. You might convert me into being a flexitarian."

The sincerity in his face told her he was telling the truth, and she was pleased. Very much so. She'd wanted him to like what she'd prepared. It had been important to her, even though she'd made life as difficult as possible for him. Even though she'd tried to keep him at arm's length, get rid of him. Even though she was afraid her feelings for him weren't simply sensual, but emotional, too.

But before she gave away too much, it was time to deflect his interest. "What about you? I know nothing about your past. You're always asking me questions."

"Questions you don't answer." A wry smile flickered over his mouth. "Not in any detail, at least."

She ignored his comment. "Tell me about yourself."

"What would you like to know?"

"I don't know." She lifted her shoulders, a helpless gesture. But she did know, really. She didn't feel comfortable coming out and asking him things directly, although she wondered why. Was it because the answers were important? His clear, green eyes met hers evenly. He was waiting.

"Okay. Where were you born? How's that for a starter?"

"L.A. That's why it was interesting to know you lived there too."

Alarm bells rang in her head, and she tensed, then tamped down her sudden fear. Perhaps he hadn't noticed. "I see. And when did you go to Chicago?"

"We left L.A. when I was a kid. My father took up a job at the University of Chicago. Physics. I suppose you could say he was married to his work rather than to his wife. Not that my mother minded. She was too busy trying to run my life." He grinned.

"Did you mind not having your father around?"

"No. I can't remember that I did. My father was the one who made knowledge come alive for me, although I was always more fascinated by history than physics. There's something so personal about studying the past, about charting human movement. And, of course, I kept up the connection with the university. I lecture there from time to time and help run the university press."

"It sounds interesting. What sort of social life do you have? Is it fun?"

"It's not really very remarkable, to tell the truth. Luckily, I have a few good friends. Other, less good ones." He told her about his interest in contemporary art, the exhibitions he'd enjoyed, and his dedication to working with and encouraging young writers.

He was easy to be with. Alice liked him more and more. She liked the enthusiasm in his voice, the passion that lit his eyes when he described things he cared about most.

"What are you really doing out here in the desert?"

"Getting the feel of the place." He leaned forward, his eyes gleaming. "You see, in my book on the history of the West, I don't want to simply write down bare facts and dates. I want to present history from the human side, take into account how people felt, how they still do feel. Take, for example, the miners who left everything behind, who believed all the exaggerated stories and outright propaganda about gold strikes, about silver, copper, and the fortune that could be made. Their misguided optimism—their hysteria—overrode normal caution, prepared them to risk—and lose—all, and for little or no reward. History happens because of emotions."

"And prejudices, and hates, and ambitions, and frustrations," added Alice and instantly felt guilty. Why always sound so negative?

Jace nodded. "That's what emotion is all about. The settling of the West was violent, ugly. But there are also many tales of kindness. Funny stories, as well."

"Tell me one," she encouraged.

"Well, take Abilene. It was once known as the wildest town in the West, and town officials had a hell of a time getting anyone to be sheriff since sheriffs rarely stayed alive for more than a few months. They finally recruited two tough-as-nails policemen from Saint Louis, Missouri, and the local cowboys decided to give them a special welcome. As their train pulled into the station, the cowboys spurred their horses into a gallop, began whooping and shooting rounds of ammunition into the air. It was Wild West chaos at its best, and the policemen watched the show from the train window. But they stayed right where they were, in their seats. Then the train pulled out, and neither man was ever seen in the area again."

Alice's laughter mingled with Jace's. It sounded good, and her heart soared. This was more fun than she'd expected. Easier. So easy. So right feeling, with the right man. The thought pulled her up short. *Cut this out, Alice Treemont. No fairy tales for you. This is a friendly dinner. No reason to think anything else is involved here. So relax.*

She did, and by the time dessert came around, Alice was regaling him with stories about Blake's Folly.

"When Robbie Sacks lost his driving license, he bought himself a curly blond wig with long ringlets. He thought the police would be fooled into believing it was his wife, Erma, behind the wheel. But they couldn't miss his full brown beard. He looked like a strange time-traveler from the court of King Louis XIV driving a battered pickup."

In what seemed like no time at all, Jace was helping her into her jacket again, and they were leaving the restaurant. How had the evening slipped by so quickly? Where had the hours gone? Deep disappointment smothered her happiness as they stood outside under a million shivering stars.

He was watching her again. He'd probably seen her disappointment. Wasn't he a man who watched her every move and noticed pretty well everything?

"What's wrong now?" he asked.

"Wrong?" She tried to give him a bright smile.

"Your face is as easy to read as the instructions on a jar of instant coffee."

"How unflattering. I've always wanted to be a woman of mystery."

"Oh, you are. You are that too. You manage to hide a lot. But not the emotions you feel."

"Phooey." She shrugged with resignation. He wouldn't let her off the hook. A man with determination was rough going. "I was enjoying myself so much," she admitted, while doubting the wisdom of her confession. "Now it's over. I feel like Cinderella climbing back into the pumpkin coach and heading back to my wicked stepmother and ugly stepsisters."

His laughter rang out again, a warm sound she was getting used to. "The dogs wouldn't like you saying that."

Was he laughing at her? She didn't care. Her rueful laughter joined his.

"Besides, who said the evening was over?"

"It isn't?" Alice stopped laughing, blinked.

"Cinderella gets a reprieve." Jace's voice was strangely gritty. "It's such hard work getting you to go anywhere, I'm not letting you escape so easily. Who knows when I'll get another chance to whisk you through the thorn barriers of your forbidding castle?"

****

The ghost town of East Brady was nothing more than five dying acacias and a jumble of shacks, most long abandoned, their weathered wooden walls slowly sliding into decay, their ever-open doors banging hopelessly in the desert wind. Only the Last Chance Saloon functioned much as it had for over a hundred and forty years. Even its decor had probably not changed much in all that time: wooden panels, gutted-looking red seats, and badly scarred tables. The place had all it needed to become a famous local landmark, and in summer, hordes of tourists filled the main room, hungry for a sentimental glimpse into the good old days. But now, out of season, the atmosphere was sleepy, timeless.

Tonight, there were a few people from Reno—easy to tell by the way they were dressed—who'd come out for the atmosphere. But there were locals, too: old-timers drank beer and played cards; a long-legged rancher, chawing a wad of tobacco, leaned indolently against a wall. Behind the bar, a dusty and ageless individual wiped glasses very slowly.

When Alice and Jace entered, everyone looked up, stared at them as they crossed the room together, like back in the restaurant.

No surprise, Jace thought. He couldn't miss the way eyes went from him, to Alice, back to him, back again to Alice. She would always draw attention, although she did so unconsciously. It was because of the way she walked, the way she held her head. And her pale, shimmering natural beauty. Here he was, as charmed as any one of the onlookers. And as strangely besotted as any teenager.

"What would you like to drink?"

"Beer," said Alice. "What else do you drink in a place like this? Beer seems to fit in."

They found a corner table and sat down. People continued to stare at them for a while, but soon the thrill of that minor activity seemed to wear off.

"Don't you mind being stared at like that all the time?" Alice whispered.

Jace blinked. "Did I hear that correctly?"

"People stare at you all the time. Back there in the restaurant. Now here. Don't you mind?"

"Alice? They're not staring at me."

"Of course they are."

"No. They're staring at us. You…and me."

"What!"

"Don't you think I noticed?"

She pulled back, wanting to deny the obvious. "No…"

"Because of the way we look together."

Her pale cheeks were touched with a delicate glow, and her eyes widened. Could the sudden softness he saw in them also contain hope? For the two of them? Jace didn't get a chance to pursue the delicious but fleeting thought.

"I know you." A man, big, burly and ugly, had appeared from nowhere. Was now leaning over their table, shaking a thick fist in Alice's face. "Bitch come messing around with my show."

"The evening's looking good," said Jace calmly. "You got a problem, buddy?"

"Bitch messing around with my show," the man hissed back. He'd obviously had a considerable amount to drink.

"Sounded as unpleasant as it did the first time," said Jace. Out of the corner of his eye, he saw Alice's face, white with anger, and her tightly clenched hands on the tabletop. "Now you can go away."

"The bitch—"

"He's talking about his lousy snake shows," interrupted Alice, with what appeared to be forced calm.

Although Jace could read signs of apprehension as well as the next person. "Snake shows?"

"The cruelest public events existing in the United States." She threw a look of disgust at the intruder.

"You keep yer nose outta where yer not wanted, lady!"

Alice turned to Jace, continued as if the man hadn't said a word. "Snakes are rounded up by spraying gasoline into their hiding places or using poles tipped with fish hooks to snare them."

"Nothing to do with you!" The man glared at her with sheer hatred.

"Oh yes, it has," replied Alice, chin defiantly in the air. "With me. And with the humane society."

"Go on," said Jace to Alice. Although why he was interested, he didn't know. He loathed snakes, but no way he'd allow anyone to frighten or hurt her. What he was now feeling was a primitive gut reaction, he knew that, all right. It was the reaction of a man who'd fight anyone who threatened his woman. *His woman*? He shoved that idea into the side of his mind. For the moment. That was something he'd deal with later.

"Once the snakes are caught," Alice continued, "they're stockpiled in crates or trashcans for months on end, without food or water. Sometimes they die. The ones who don't are brought to shows where they are dropped onto concrete floors, putted with golf clubs, or used in sacking contests. That means being bent in half and put into a sack over and over again. During those hideous games, the snakes have their ribs and jaws broken. And that's all done in the name of fun and sport."

"That's what people pay to see. They're vermin, snakes are. Vermin!" The man leaned in closer, and an unpleasant stink of alcohol and sweat hung over the table.

Alice grimaced and turned to Jace again. "Joe here specializes in offering tourists the chance to have their photos taken with rattlesnakes in his show. The jaws of the snake are sewn together so that they can't do any harm. In the end, all the snakes are killed. Beheaded. That way, everybody can have a good laugh because the severed heads retain signs of consciousness for up to an hour and a half. They even try to bite when they're tormented by their handlers."

"Ugly," said Jace slowly. He wished this jerk Joe would vanish. They hadn't needed his disgusting interference. "Sounds like the thing that happened in county fairs in the old days. Before anyone thought of protecting animals."

"People get what they pay their money for," Joe jeered. "You and yer lousy friends keep away from me and my business!"

"You're repeating yourself, Joe." Jace stood, felt Alice's restraining hand on his arm. "Don't worry, Alice. Joe was about to leave."

He wasn't. Not immediately. Swaying, staring aggressively, the man sensed Jace was no pushover. And he finally turned, lurched away into another section of the saloon.

Jace stared after him for a minute until certain he wouldn't return.

"Jace?"

He unclenched his jaw. He hated violence of any sort, but if pushed, wouldn't back out. He looked down at Alice. "You didn't tell me going out with you was going to be a Wild West adventure."

She frowned. "Sorry."

"What are you sorry for? If that's really what snake shows are about, I'm on your side. I don't like cruelty any more than you do." He held out her jacket. "How

87

about if we head back to Blake's Folly. I think we've milked this social occasion for all it's worth."

As he led her back out into the cool starry night, he wondered at himself, at Alice, at the sudden change in his perception of snakes, those same creatures he'd despised this morning. Life could certainly pull some strange punches.

****

Here was the house, the dusty path, and the front porch. Soon they'd be walking up the stairs to the first floor, in the direction of their bedrooms. Would he kiss her again like this morning? The thought made her shiver. With fear? Or anticipation? Or deep-down knockout desire.

"Feel like sitting out on the porch for a while?"

"Sure."

The tired old settee groaned under their weight, and the night air held that touch of frost that warned them not to get too comfortable.

Jace reached out, linked her fingers through his. The warmth flowed up through her arm, right to her heart, like some rich, sweet liqueur.

"Thanks," she said.

"For what?" He watched her, a curious smile playing over his mouth.

"For a lovely evening. And for helping me out back there, in the saloon."

"You're joking, aren't you? No man messes around with any woman I'm with." It was said lightly. Casually.

Alice couldn't let it lie there. "Any woman? How about a wife? Is there a wife out there somewhere?" The question surprised her. It had slid out from somewhere in her unconscious before she'd thought of the possibility of Jace being married.

There was utter silence for several tense moments. Devastated, Alice looked out at the desert night. So. There was someone. He was a married man. He wasn't free. She'd been letting herself dream about a man who was on the lookout for a quick and very illicit affair.

"Alice? Look at me."

She couldn't. If she did, he'd be able to see her disappointment. Her anger. Despite the darkness of the desert night.

"Look at me!" It was an order. His hand dropped hers. Reaching out, he cupped her chin, forced her to turn her head, meet his gaze. He wasn't smiling. Not anymore.

"You think I'm the sort of man who'd have asked you out if I had a wife somewhere?" He sounded angry. Until another note insinuated itself into his voice, one that was husky, intense. "The sort who would kiss you like I did last night, or this morning, knowing I had a wife who would be hurt by it?"

Relief wrangled with confusion. She wanted to stand up and sing; she wanted to run away as quickly as she could. Instead, she forced herself to sound cold, cynical. Realistic. "Things like that have been known to happen. Often enough."

His hand released her chin, and his voice was as cool as her own. "Well, not with me. Never with me. Remember that."

She'd made him angry, she realized. She'd questioned his honesty, and that had wounded him. But how could she have known? They'd met such a short time ago. And even when you knew someone for a long, long time, knew them intimately, lived with them, slept beside them, ate breakfast and dinner with them, you couldn't be certain of their fidelity. Experience had taught her that very lesson.

Then she forced back the painful memories, ones that were intruding from another life—the one that had ended long ago. She forced herself to smile. "Sorry for having doubted you. So why haven't you ever married?"

He looked out into the night. "When I was younger, I was waiting for a meeting with a kindred spirit, as idealistic as that sounds. A woman with the same beliefs, attitudes, and values as I had. That was very important since I never planned on getting married more than once."

He was right, Alice mused. "Living with someone day in and day out can be difficult enough, but if you don't have the same morals and ideals, marriage is hell."

"Absolute hell." He paused briefly. Wanting to know more, yet worried that she would resist, bring this trusting moment to an end? "I've observed how bad things can get. Now that I'm older and know myself better, I realize how wise my early decision was."

"Especially since we do tend to become more intractable with age."

He looked relieved. That they were on the same wavelength? "That's very true. There were several times in my life when I thought I was about to fall in love...then the feeling simply wore off. As soon as babies, and mortgages, and full commitment, came into the picture. Particularly the expectation that I change to fit into someone else's picture of how I should be. And adhere to time schedules that meant the end of personal choice. And requests that I be around more, spend less time writing, or investigating, or traveling, or pursuing subjects that fascinate me."

"Oh yes, I know all about that," said Alice, leaning forward. "And because you don't give in to other people's demands on your time, everyone tells you how self-centered you are. How egoistic. How selfish. And how downright boring you are because you feel passionately about an unusual subject, one that doesn't fit into cocktail party situations."

His eyes searched hers warily. "Yes, I've heard those recriminations many times."

Alice laughed shortly. "I'll bet you have."

He smiled back, but his expression was guarded. "How do you know this? Is it the sort of thing you say?"

"Never." She punched the settee's seat vehemently. "Oh no, not me. Those accusations would never cross my lips, mainly because I've had them thrown at me all my life, and I know how exasperating they can be."

Now he relaxed, and the smile spread into a grin. "This is getting better and better. We must both be aliens from the same distant planet."

"Jupiter? Saturn?"

"Much farther, I think. From another galaxy altogether."

Their eyes locked, and the little thrill of fear raced up her spine again. She was so close to him this very instant. No doubt it was the same for him too. A bond had been forged between them tonight. Now what would happen…would she follow him upstairs, take him to her bed as she longed to do and let him become part of her life? Then wonder if she'd ever see him again after he returned to Chicago. Because his return was imminent, therefore separation would never be far off.

No, she couldn't live like that. If she made love with

him, she would give her whole heart, her soul, to Jace. Already, she felt too much, took too much pleasure in his every glance, his gestures, in the conversations they shared, in his natural warmth. She loved hearing his ideas, appreciated his open-mindedness, and adored his sense of humor. How easy it would be to fall in love with Jace, and how would that end? In heartbreak. In the sort of pain she never wanted to experience again. That left her with no choice: she had to destroy the intimacy of this moment. Immediately.

"So in Chicago you live the bachelor life." Her voice sounded tight, jagged, to her own ears. "One affair after another, no strings attached."

"I guess you could say that's a fairly good description of the landscape of my romantic life up until now," he answered lazily. "Although it sounds banal and rather unappealing when put like that."

Up until now? What did that mean? Anything at all? Anything personal? Of course not, although she wished it did. And knew she couldn't allow herself to think that way. He was a playboy, pure and simple. She knew the type, knew the havoc they wreaked. Far too well. "Is there one woman you see more than others back in Chicago?"

His glance was probing. "Is it important to have this conversation right now?"

"I thought this was called getting to know each other better. That's what you suggested, isn't it?"

"If that's the way you want it." His voice held no great enthusiasm. "I see several women. There's one, Tanya, I go out with fairly often."

Tanya. Of course. A woman with a name like Tanya. No Linda, or Sue, or Joan, for Jace. Nope. But

Tanya...the name conjured up sleek sophistication, perfume. She'd be exotic and utterly beautiful. Phooey. Alice hated her.

At least now she knew the way the wind was blowing. Jace Constant had decided to have a short affair with her, something lusty that would tide him over until he got home and back into Tanya's arms. The thought left a bittersweet taste in her mouth. Should she be pleased or offended? And why had he chosen her, Alice, a woman with no glamour, a recluse, for his affair? For a little something on the original side, she told herself, yet again.

Jace raised his hand, let his fingers slowly trace the fine line of her cheekbone, the contour of her lips, conjuring up a wild trail of sparks, a hum of desire, a yearning for more that—almost—erased the pain of her thoughts.

Alice pulled back, away from his touch. "Jace, listen..."

"I'm here."

She sat up straight, prepared to destroy all. "I like you, really I do. I like your company."

He wasn't in the least perturbed. "And this is the beginning."

"What beginning? I'm actually very different from you, no matter what you say. I don't have short affairs. Ever. Besides..." She took a deep breath before telling the lie. "I also have someone in my life." She watched his smile vanish.

"Who?"

"Brad."

"Brad?"

"A rancher. From Two Posts." She hoped Jace and

Brad never met up. If they did, the game would be up. But when would they meet? Jace would be out of here in no time.

"Brad. The Rancher from Two Posts," Jace repeated. "I feel like I've strolled into a bad Western."

"Oh, I do understand. You see how different we are? Brad's a rough-and-ready type of guy. Ever so Western. Doesn't at all fit into the same sort of picture frame as your Tanya with her exotic perfume, designer clothing, and sexy boudoir." She forced an arch smile.

"Boudoir?" Jace's eyebrow quirked with amusement; his eyes glittered. "How gorgeously archaic."

"Or whatever." Okay, she'd gone too far. Alice felt like kicking herself. "I threw in the boudoir image for contrast, you see."

"Of course. I understand." He was obviously trying not to laugh out loud.

"What I meant to say is that Brad is the opposite. Tall, lean. A real outdoors man. One who loves the desert."

"And snakes, of course."

"Well," said Alice judiciously, "I can't say he's as fond of them as I am." No, she certainly couldn't. When Alice had discovered battered snake cadavers on his land, she'd wiped Brad off the screen of her life. Until this moment, when he was needed as the first line of defense. Against Jace. Against her attraction. Her emotions.

"Do you love him?" Jace asked.

Alice stared back, wide-eyed, wordless. Now what would she do? Say she was madly in love? No, she couldn't do that. That would be going too far. Even now.

Fighting for time, she stood, took a few steps in the direction of the front door. Then turned, looked back at Jace. And in the best, overly theatrical way she could possibly manage, she opened her arms in a wide, woman-of-the-world gesture. "Love! Oh, does that silly little word really mean anything at all?"

As she slipped into the house, she was well aware she'd sounded like a bad actress in a tenth-rate play. But, then again, that was an experience not totally unknown to her. Once upon a time.

Chapter Eight

The Charm Plan

"The Charm Plan," murmured Jace to himself with a smirk of satisfaction. Leaning back against the counter, he basked in a dancing beam of sunlight while coffee filtered lazily into the pot. Alice hadn't made an appearance this morning, and there was no sign of breakfast. Therefore, reasoned Jace, she must be in her bed, sleeping. He grinned. Good. That showed him fate was on his side, nodding with approval at the Charm Plan.

What was the Plan exactly? It was an excellent idea. It was an almost-sure method for knocking rivals out of the scene, rivals like that Brad what's-his-name from Two Posts—if Brad really did exist. Because, Jace reasoned, where is dear, old Rancher Brad? *He certainly never shows his nose around here.* Alice never seemed to go out on mysterious dates, either. So, was Rancher Brad really and truly a serious rival? He doubted it.

Those were the thoughts that had kept him awake half the night. And that was how he'd conceived the Plan. It was simple, easy to put into motion. It consisted of keeping things as cool as he possibly could with Alice until she came to the conclusion that he was irresistible. She was attracted to him. He knew it, could feel it, could see it in the way she looked at him, even if she refused to acknowledge or accept that. Look how she kept on shoving up barriers between the two of them.

No, the Charm Plan was the only way to win Alice that he could figure out. If that didn't work, well, he'd have to invent something else. Why? He wanted her. She fascinated him. He loved being with her, talking to her. He...

The coffee was ready. Jace filled a large cup and headed back upstairs. Pausing in the hallway outside of Alice's bedroom, he listened. Not a sound. Did she lock her door at night? He held his breath and turned the knob. No, she didn't. His heart gave a satisfied little thump. She trusted him...to a certain extent, at least.

For a minute or two, Jace simply stood in the open doorway, waiting until his eyes got used to the dim light and things could form into shapes. Those furry lumps on the floor around the bed were dogs because their tails were flapping softly in their usual cheery welcome. As for the rest, he had been so astonished by Alice's loveliness yesterday evening he hadn't had time to take it all in. Now he did.

The large square room was touched by soft pastel and shadow and filled with ancient pieces of furniture, most of them covered with books. Jace smiled. He could imagine Alice spending long dark winter evenings in here, reading by the light of that bedside lamp. Yes, that would be a nice way to pass evenings, all right, on that bed with Alice beside him.

No. His thoughts were going in a dangerous direction. *Cool down.* She was there, in that big four-poster bed, right now. Without him. Sound asleep, lying under a pale silken counterpane, head turned slightly to one side, her arms flung out beside her in the innocent way of a child. Her tangle of shining hair spread out over the pillows, down over her naked shoulders. He approached, fascinated.

How peaceful she looked, how lovely, like a princess in a fairy tale. The princess condemned to sleep until the prince found her and woke her with a kiss.

Carefully, he put the coffee cup down on the wooden night table between two piles of books. A kiss? The Plan didn't include kissing. However, like all good plans, rules didn't have to be followed strictly to the letter. There had to be some leeway.

He bent down and kissed her gently. Beautiful lips, he thought. Irresistible.

Like a fairy tale princess, her lids fluttered, and she abandoned sleep. Her eyes opened, and she found him standing there. The softest, most tender expression crossed her face. Was he the one caught in slumber's fantasy world? No, he wasn't. But a swell of joy filled his heart, astonishing him. Those first sleepy seconds had told him the truth about her feelings. She hadn't had time to hide, be defensive.

"Jace! I was dreaming about you."

His knees weakened. "If the dreams you're having about me are anything like the ones I have about you, Princess, it's a miracle you manage to sleep at all."

Then he felt like kicking himself! The Charm Plan didn't allow him to say things like that, even if they were true.

"Princess? You called me Princess?" She stared at him, her eyes full of tenderness, astonishment. And then, as if a horribly unpleasant thought suddenly seared across her mind, the softness vanished. "What are you doing here in my bedroom?" She shot to a sitting position. Or almost did. Immediately, she clutched at the sheet and crossed her arms in front of her.

Which is when Jace realized the significance of the naked shoulders. He grinned wickedly. "Alice Treemont, you astound me."

She met his gaze with embarrassed defiance. "Now what have I done?"

"You sleep naked," he said simply. "That's a very exciting idea." Impossible to keep the huskiness out of his voice. Damn it. The Plan was being shot to hell. Because if there was one thing he longed to do more than anything else was to take those lips of hers again, to pry that sheet out of her hands, to fold it back and reveal her nakedness. He wanted to see her, to see her breasts, kiss their tips, trace a line to her belly with his mouth, go lower, deeper, kiss every inch of her.

He pulled himself back sharply. The thought of what he'd like to be doing with Alice caused an almost uncontrollable jolt of desire to shoot through him. His fingers twitched, wanting to touch, to caress. But he couldn't do that.

Instead, he reached for the coffee cup, offered it to her. "Hot and freshly made. Milk and no sugar, the way you like it." With great effort he managed to control his face, keep it devoid of expression.

Which was more than could be said for Alice. In the dim light, her cheeks were a fiery pink. As if one of her deep dark secrets had been found out. "What's wrong with sleeping in the nude? And why do I have to justify myself? This is too much! First you invade my house, now you invade my bedroom."

"I'm waiting for you to take this cup." The rich smell of hot fresh coffee wafted through the air.

She opened her mouth, closed it again, as if seeing the uselessness of argument. Holding the sheet tightly against her breasts with one hand, she leaned back against the pillows, reached out for the cup with the other. Her mouth curved upward. "It's awfully nice of you to bring me coffee in bed. Milk and no sugar. How did you notice such a banal detail?"

"How people like their coffee is no banal detail."

"Okay." The smile became a grin. "And, by the way, what are you doing up so early?"

"Early? It's ten o'clock."

"Ten!" Her eyes opened wide. "Impossible. I never sleep until ten. I have to get up and make your breakfast! You're always out of the house by this time." She reached to put her cup on the table, but he stopped her movement.

"I'm not going anywhere. I'm taking the day off. And I'm in charge of breakfast this morning. It'll be waiting for you in the kitchen."

"Jace. No."

"If you go argue with the wind, it'll be just as useful!" he said, heading for the door. "Drink your coffee and luxuriate. Be happy you have a slave for once."

He was feeling inordinately pleased. By the look of it, he'd won a battle. Not the war, of course, not yet. Still, the Charm Plan seemed to be the best thing to hit civilization since fine Kentucky bourbon.

****

Twenty minutes later, the sound of loud banging had Alice shooting down the stairs and out through the front door. What was going on? It sounded as if a whole wrecking crew was slugging away at the very walls of her house. Any second now, the whole entire building would collapse into a vast heap of dust and shattered sticks of furniture.

She found Jace sitting on the ground beside the veranda, nails sticking out of his mouth, a hammer in his hand and a stack of thick old wooden beams beside him. Now what was this absolutely infuriating person up to? He wasn't going to make her life miserable all day long, was he? Yes, it looked like he was.

"What do you think you're doing?"

He turned his head, gazed at her nonchalantly. Took the nails out of his mouth and whistled lasciviously. "Jeans. I didn't know you owned a pair of jeans. I like your hair like that, too."

She blushed. She'd pinned her hair back in a low, loose chignon but would rather have been eaten by ants than admit she'd taken special care with her appearance this morning. Why? Because she really did want to please him. "Jace, I want an answer. What are you doing?"

"Didn't anyone ever tell you a house needs upkeep? If you want this place to be standing in another one hundred and fifty years, there are things that have to be done. Urgently. This joist here, for example. It needs to be reinforced, so I'm doing that."

"You've no right!" She leaned forward aggressively, hands balled into fists.

His eyes twinkled. "A man likes to catch up on home repairs on his day off."

"This is my house, not yours!"

"Quite right. You own the house. But, at the moment, this happens to be my home." He put a nail into place and banged away at it.

All Alice could do was stand there, wait patiently

for the noise to stop so she could continue the argument. God, he was infuriating. "It isn't your home! Your home is in Chicago."

"My apartment is in Chicago. That's true enough. A nice, big, flashy apartment with expensive, modern furniture. I've also worked out that it's perfectly impersonal and soulless. Simply an apartment, get it? Not a home. This place is a home. A real home. And I feel like helping you protect it." He began attacking another nail. Stopped. Looked at her. "And when I'm finished with this job, the veranda isn't going to cave in like it was threatening to do. And, by the way, I'm not stopping with the veranda. There's all the rest." The wide gesture he made encompassed the whole house, the yard, the road, all of Blake's Folly.

"The entire state of Nevada," Alice muttered sourly and glared ferociously, hoping he'd eventually take the hint or feel intimidated. But since he didn't bother looking up again, her effort was wasted. Besides, he was right, and he was doing her a big favor. He might be gone in a few weeks' time, but the veranda wouldn't be.

She turned to go back into the house.

"Alice?"

She stopped. "Now what?" She forced herself to look forbidding.

He stood, brushed off his pants. "Breakfast is waiting. After that, we'll take the dogs for a walk. Together. I'd like you to show me more of the desert."

"No way." What would he come up with next? What was he trying to do? Run a revolution? "I go on my walks alone."

"Not today, you aren't. I bought a pair of walking boots like yours, and today's the day I'll be testing them." His eyes twinkled mischievously. "Besides, it's Saturday, and I promised Killer we'd go walking on Saturday. Can't disappoint Killer like that, Princess. Could mess up his psyche."

"Why are you calling me Princess?" she asked suspiciously.

His grin broadened. "Private joke."

"Between you and who else? Killer?" Exasperated, Alice stomped back into the house, but not before she heard him coming up behind her and whistling a vaguely familiar tune. What was that melody? She searched her mind. The words rushed into her head: "You'll never walk alone."

No. He really was pushing things too far. Making fun of her too. Not that there was anything she could do about it. More useful for her to concentrate, get on with her life—as if she could with all the ruckus that man was creating.

****

"Which way are we walking?" Jace asked when dishes had been washed and put away. They'd eaten together, of course. So that problem had been resolved. Now he waited for her protests about the walk to begin again.

"Hangman's Hill," she answered calmly, as if there'd never been the slightest opposition to his accompanying her.

"Sounds cheery."

They went out onto the veranda, where Alice whistled for the dogs and attached them on leashes.

"Are you afraid they'll run off, become strays again?"

"That's the least of my worries!" Her mouth twisted

103

into a wry grimace. "Most dogs know when they've got a good thing going for them. I usually manage to find good homes for some and keep the ones that no one will adopt."

"So why the leashes?"

"So they won't run wild and hunt. I let them off when I'm sure the coast is clear."

Of course, thought Jace. He should have thought of that. Trust Alice to be softhearted about any living creature—with the exception of Jace Constant.

"Then I suppose you'll be interested to learn that there's a good chance the Winterback Mine area will be turned into a conservation area, park, and wildlife refuge."

Alice nodded but with less enthusiasm than he'd expected. "So I've heard. But, so far, that's little more than rumor. The politicians have to agree to the project, and funding needs to be found. Those are two huge hurdles."

"But it might happen."

"It might, yes. But how will the land be used? Will it become a real and badly needed refuge for wildlife or a weak concession that opens a natural area to destructive tourism complete with mountain bikes, e-bikes, high-powered snow bikes, and dune buggies?"

He fell into step beside her as they set off on a dirt road behind the house, one that led over a dusty rise and onto a bare plain of rock formations, a scrabble of ill-looking bushes, and fissured earth flats. "I see your point. But wouldn't it be advantageous to have people with your sort of knowledge and awareness on site to ward off the worst destruction?" Once again, he admired the way she moved, her long, healthy, slightly awkward stride. It was good to be walking beside her like this; their steps had the same range, the same swing, as if they were meant to cross the world together. It felt right.

He also liked the way the wind fluttered the loose strands of hair that had escaped from her chignon. Still, the expression on her face hadn't softened. Not really. She looked as proud, as defiant as ever. Not the way she'd looked at him when he'd stood by her bed this morning. He almost smiled. That had been her secret face, the one he wanted to see again. And he would. He was determined he would.

"Do you have an ulterior motive in taking me to a place called Hangman's Hill?"

She laughed. "Is your conscience bothering you?"

"Why? Forcing my company on you doesn't seem like a very serious crime."

"Actually no one knows why it's called that—especially since the old gallows where cattle rustlers and horse thieves were hanged is on the other side of Blake's Folly. There aren't even any gruesome stories about this place. Except one."

"I figured there did have to be at least one." He shook his head in mock resignation.

Her clear eyes sparkled as they met his, and his heart swelled. Special. The word floated lazily through his head.

"Okay, it's not horribly gruesome," she conceded. "As you probably know, winters here can be terribly harsh. One year, when spring thaw came, someone from the village found a frozen cow out there. At first, everyone thought it had died of starvation. Until they discovered a cowboy, alive and fairly warm, inside the dead animal. He'd been out of work like most cowboys were in the winter and had nowhere to live. When the weather became very cold, he'd killed the cow and crawled into its corpse to survive."

"Lesson number one in desert survival," said Jace. "I'll keep it in mind until summer comes around." Now what had he said? Summer? That was months and months away. What was he talking about? He wasn't going to be anywhere around here then. Had Alice noticed the slipup? He didn't think so.

"I often think of those migrants who came to towns like Blake's Folly, a hundred, a hundred and fifty years ago," she was saying. "Most came from poor areas in Europe, or big cities in the east, and they trudged all across the country hoping for independence, the right to own land and support their large families."

"And, for the first time, having land that their sons could inherit."

"Yes, that's true. But if you read the old diaries, it was the men who were enthusiastic about the great adventure of traveling through wild places, encountering so-called savage Indians, and hunting buffalo to near extinction. Most women hated the seemingly endless days of walking and unending toil that was always their everyday lot. They also resented leaving homes, friends, and families behind and having no right to question decisions made for them by husbands and fathers. At least when the gold rush and silver boom began, the men left their women behind when they came out here because they were planning on getting rich, not settling."

"Where did you learn so much local history? From living here?" Jace asked.

"I read. Books exist in Blake's Folly, in case you didn't notice."

"Oh, I noticed, all right," he said, amused. "There are heaps of books all over your bedroom. You probably spend a lot of time reading in bed."

"And?"

"So do I," he said softly. Once again, the thought conjured up nights with Alice in that big bed of hers. Reading. And doing other things…

They had reached the top of a high hill, and Jace looked around. Straggling Blake's Folly was far behind them, and as far as the eye could see, everything was beige: the wide beige valley in front of them, the range of bare beige hills in the distance. "Strange place," he murmured. "Like the surface of the moon."

"In a way. But I really do love it here. It's gorgeous."

Although he couldn't agree with the aesthetic, he did like the passion she put into her declaration. *A passionate woman.* Believing passionately in causes. Feeling passionate about a landscape. Reacting with passion when he touched her. Very nice, very rare. As rare as pure gold. And he'd found it here. His feeling of satisfaction curled up nicely with his raw desire.

"Any rattlesnakes out this way?"

"Worried?" she asked.

"Cautious. I'm counting on you to pull me through this."

"I'll do my best." She looked at him. "But why worry about rattlesnakes now? Because you're in the desert? There are rattlers everywhere. In the eastern states, in California. They're wonderful swimmers too: they push against the water. People have spotted them several miles offshore. And some climb trees."

The subject wasn't a pleasant one to him, but for some reason, he was feeling less queasy than he usually did. Alice was watching him closely, and he forced himself to smile. More than anything, he didn't want to look like a weak coward in her eyes.

"Are you all right talking about this?" she asked.

"Fine. Perhaps the more familiar I become with the subject, the less traumatic it will be. Nonetheless, I'd like to make a deal. I charm you; you charm the snakes."

She laughed and held out her hand to seal the bargain. He curled it into his and felt like a king. Savoring the moment, he breathed in deeply and the air was dry, strangely pungent in a harsh, unusual way. "I might actually start to appreciate this part of the world," he said, surprising himself completely.

Her grin was smug. "You see. The place grows on you little by little. When I first came back here, I thought I'd made the crazy decision to live on an asteroid. I'd spend days walking up around these hills, searching for something that was different, something alive, something green—a forest, a garden, a lawn, a hedge— anything at all. But all I could find was one colorless valley with a rim of hills leading on to another colorless valley."

"You stuck it out. Came to love the area."

"I did. I was lucky, though. Not everyone inherits a grand old house. I'd have been a pretty ungrateful wretch to have snubbed a gift like that."

He waited, hoped she would confide in him, tell him more. But she didn't. Unless he pried, and he now knew how much she hated that. Still, he couldn't stop himself. "You must have wanted to get away from something pretty badly."

Her eyes avoided his, but she nodded. "Oh, yes. I was definitely running away."

"From?"

"From everything. From a life I hated."

"From a man?"

Her eyes met his, finally. Her lip curled. "Also from a man. My husband, as it happens. The world's greatest playboy."

"I see," said Jace.

"I suppose you do." Her eyes challenged him. "Don't you go in for the same billing?"

"Billing?"

"As a consummate playboy."

Jace raised both hands in denial. "Oh no, Alice. That's unfair. I thought I already made it clear I'd never be a playboy husband. Never. And as for calling me a playboy, well, that's your label, not mine."

Although, when he remembered the conversation they'd had on the veranda last night, the designation didn't sound that far off the mark.

****

The easiest way back to the house led through the middle of Blake's Folly. By now, the sun had disappeared behind a deep veil of cloud, and a gentler light blurred the bleak landscape, softening the snaggle of ramshackle dwellings, caravans, and shacks, lending them a mysterious but strangely homey air.

Jace seemed to be particularly interested in a huge pile of boards stacked up in a yard that would never, under any circumstances, be called a garden. True, there were a few long-dead and stringy flowers in tubs, several gasping, scraggly, and leafless trees, but most of the space was taken up by pans, boilers, tires, car parts, and unknown metal carcasses that might—a very long time ago—have belonged to something recognizable.

"If I didn't know I was in Blake's Folly, I'd say we were looking at contemporary art in a sculpture park," said Jace, the amusement evident in his voice.

Alice stole a glance at him from under her eyelashes, at the strong jaw, the fine lines crinkling around the shining green eyes. Too late to tamp down her feelings for him. Jace had penetrated every secret place in her heart, and there was no going back. All she could do was hide what she felt. She managed to sound calm, slightly mocking. "Funny. I've never thought of Pa Handy as an artist before. I wonder what Ma would say about that. She thinks Pa's going to clear this mess away one day. She wants to plant a rose garden."

"A rose garden? In the desert?"

"You can't stay married to Pa Handy and not be a little crazy."

"Does he sell any of this stuff?"

"Would anybody want to buy it?" Alice scoffed.

"Yup. I would."

Jace swung open a rusty gate and headed along a path leading through the rubble and up to the bungalow door.

Alice followed him with a definite feeling of dread. "You don't want to do this," she whispered desperately. "Ma Handy's the biggest gossip in Blake's Folly."

"I can survive that. Blake's Folly has a population of fifty-four these days, if you count me in."

"She'll imagine all sorts of things if we come calling together."

"So?"

"So? Jace, listen!"

He didn't.

The door whipped open before he had a chance to

knock. Alice cringed. Ma had probably been observing them for the last half hour via some secret and highly illegal telemetric device complete with sensor and transmission path detector.

"Why, Alice, what a nice surprise. Come in, come in both of you. Take off your coats, make yourselves at home." Ma's eyes glittered as they unashamedly took Jace in from head to toe.

"We won't be staying, Ma," said Alice trying to prepare a quick escape. In another minute, she figured Ma would be asking Jace exactly what his intentions were. "Jace wanted to ask Pa a question." But Alice realized she was talking to herself. Ma had already linked her arm through Jace's and was drawing him into a tiny overheated living room crowded with stranger objects than those out in the yard.

"Of course, you're Jace Constant, Alice's new lodger. I've been hearing so much about you." Ma Handy never did beat about the bush when on an information-gathering mission.

Alice's groan was barely audible, but Jace caught it. She could see by his sparkling eyes that he was actually enjoying himself.

"Welcome, both of you," shouted Pa from a monstrous armchair in one corner of the room. On a low table in front of him were what looked to be around a thousand bolts, nuts, screws, springs, and wires. "Company's exactly what we need. I'm having no luck putting this whoosits together anyway. Sure gets on my nerves."

"What is that whoosits actually supposed to be, Pa?" Alice asked weakly, her mind desperately whirling, searching for a safe subject of conversation. There was no telling what embarrassing things Ma would come up with when she had a mind to being obnoxiously nosy.

"Dunno, really," said Pa scratching his head. "Little thing I picked up over Dulverton way, sitting out there on a pile of junk I went to see. Thought if I tinkered around a bit, it'd come to something."

Search as she might, Alice couldn't come up with a snappy response to that.

Ma Handy was still staring at Jace, though. She wasn't going to let him off the hook now that he was in her lair. If anyone had a one-track mind, it sure was Ma.

"You're a good-looking man, too. Robust, nice and healthy," Ma now said. "I mentioned to Jane Grimes yesterday, that I thought it was about time Alice here had a little company in that big old mansion of hers. I don't know, but I'd be scared out of my wits out there all on my very own with no one within shouting distance."

"Ma—" began Alice, but there was no stopping the flow.

"You seem to be a man who can hold up his end of the conversation, and some folks are saying you've made a name for yourself. That must be a comfort for Alice. You're the kind of man she needs to have around."

Alice wished with all her might that the ground would open up under her feet or—even better—under Ma's. Of course it didn't: you never could rely on natural phenomena when you needed them. She didn't dare shoot a miserable glance in Jace's direction. What could he be thinking?

"Of course, Alice," continued Pa, inexorably following Ma's deft probing. "Good looks don't matter at all when you meet the right person. Nor age, neither. Look at me. I'm a good six years older than Ma."

"You'd never know it," Jace confirmed, his face perfectly deadpan.

It was true. Pa looked pretty much like Ma. Both of them were shapeless, ageless, and shameless.

"Now, it's lunchtime, so you'll both sit down with us, have a bowl of soup, a sandwich or two, a cup of coffee and a piece of pie," said Ma.

"No, Ma. Thanks, but—" Alice might as well have saved her breath.

"Of course you will. Fresh apple pie. Baked it early this morning. No one's walking out that door without having a taste of it."

Even if it had to be at gunpoint.

"I was wondering if you wanted to sell some of the wood you have outside," Jace said to Pa as he moved over to the table and took the seat Ma offered him. "Some of the paneling on the side of Alice's house needs replacing, and I could get it done in a few hours if I had the boards."

"Jace—" Alice began again, then stopped.

Ma was gaping at her. "Alice. Don't tell me this delightful man is fixing up that old dump of yours. Well, that's mighty nice of him."

"Yes," muttered Alice. "Isn't that what good-looking, healthy, robust, and successful men are for?" But sarcasm was wasted on Ma, who'd never recognize it in a million years. What Alice really wanted to do, of course, was rant, stamp her foot, tell Jace he'd done enough already. That it was, after all, *her* house, *her* property, *her* life. Yet she knew how hopeless her position was. She certainly couldn't win in the face of Jace's determination. Or Ma's.

Right now, Ma was memorizing every single word

of the conversation, and before tomorrow's dawn cracked, every single soul in Blake's Folly, living or dead, would have heard a totally adulterated and highly dramatic version of it. And they'd be cooking up a deeply satisfying, totally incorrect love story as well. One with a happy end, of course.

That's all she needed. To be the center of everyone's attention. And what would they all be saying when Jace picked up and left? Went roaring back to Chicago, to the good life? To Tanya? That she, poor Alice, was too much of a crank to be able to hold on to a man for any longer than a few short weeks?

Phooey.

Chapter Nine

The Tactic

At nine fifteen the next morning, a horrendous grinding noise, comparable to that of an ancient dump truck on a corrugated tin roof, was heard on the road. It was the arrival of Pa Handy's old pickup, delivering the wood Jace had purchased from him. After that there was no easy way of getting rid of Pa; he stuck around like rubber glue, feigning interest in Jace's home improvement scheme but, in reality, on another fact-finding mission. No doubt Ma had told him to come back with some new juicy gossip—or else. When Alice caught the silly, sheepish look on Pa's face, she knew her suspicions were right.

Knowing that the slightest comment she made to Jace or the tiniest look in his direction was bound to be misinterpreted, she decided the best defense against an attack of local curiosity was to remain safe and sound in her study. Not that she was able to get any work done. Her territory had been invaded by two males, and she was fuming like one of her own badly cracked woodstoves. Besides, the conversation the men were having outside—if such a thing could be called conversation—was impossible to block out.

"Fixing up the old veranda, eh?"

"That's right."

"Sure does need fixing up. Everyone here in town's been saying that for years."

Jace's answer to that was a volley of hammering. Pa, however, was a patient and determined individual when he had to be. He waited for the next pause.

"Take you years to fix this here whole place up. Yep, years. You thinking of doing all that?"

"Depends what you mean by fixing up."

Jace had hedged that one nicely, thought Alice with a grim, masochistic sort of satisfaction.

"Well, at least a year or two, or perhaps three. Think you'll be around that long?"

If Jace had answered, Alice wasn't able to hear over the hammering. Finally, after an eternity or two, the dump truck whipped up a cloud of dust and carbon monoxide that violently and completely blocked out the cerulean sky, then moved back over the corrugated tin roof in the direction of home.

Now, finally, Alice dared to make an appearance. Jace was sizing up the work to be done on the eastern wall. This was crazy, it really was. Why was he willing to put so much work into a house that wasn't his? It wasn't as if things were really steamy between the two of them.

Take what had happened yesterday. After they'd come home from Pa and Ma Handy's, Jace had hammered until dark. In the evening? Spicy bean stew, a bottle of wine in the kitchen, easy conversation about the research Jace was doing. Nothing else. What had she expected? Steamy kisses? More of that passion she knew was so near to the surface? But he'd made no move to touch her. He'd yawned, finally, and said it was time to turn in.

Well, she wasn't going to beg him to stay up with her, was she? Of course not. She wasn't going to put her arms around him and kiss him again the way she had done before. Certainly not. Not when he showed nothing but indifference.

They'd climbed the stairway to go to their bedrooms. Five sleepy dogs followed.

"Like a shepherd with his flock," Jace had said, his voice light, jocular.

Alice's heart had been beating wildly with the intimacy of the simple act of being on the steps together in the dark of the night. But when they finally reached the landing, Jace had simply bent over her, kissed her gently on the forehead. A nice gesture. A friendly one. The gesture of one good chum to another.

"Good night, Alice."

She had stared up at him, but he'd looked relaxed and mild. And impersonal.

"Good night, Jace," she'd managed to say, also keeping her voice polite-sounding, cool, calm. Not betraying the craving raging through her, not giving away her confusion.

"Sleep well."

"You too."

He'd turned and, with a little half wave, had gone into his room. She'd walked down the long corridor leading to her room, her heart heavy.

So this was it, then. She'd ruined everything. It had been entirely her fault. She was the one who had invented the totally fictional romance with Brad the Rancher. Because she'd been jealous of an unknown woman named Tanya.

Or perhaps that wasn't the reason Jace seemed so

indifferent. Perhaps he'd decided he didn't want her anymore, that a lightning-quick affair with her wasn't worth all the effort. So why did she feel so miserable? Isn't this what she'd asked for? Demanded, even! She should be grateful. And relieved. Danger had been avoided.

Then why was Jace out here again this morning? Why was he working on her house? What would he get out of this? She had to know. She stepped out into the yard. "Look, Jace, how about if I help?"

Jace looked up from the wood he was contemplating. "I don't need your help. Two people doing this would constitute a crowd." He bent over one of the boards, measured it.

Alice continued to stand there, watching the way his body moved. There was a slight tear in his jeans. Why did she have the sudden impulse to move in closer, lean down and touch his leg, right there? Feel his skin between the slits of fabric? She couldn't miss the way his muscles worked, either. His arms in the rolled-back sleeves were smooth, strong, wonderful-looking. *Stop drooling*!

"Jace, I can't let you do this alone! It makes me feel so guilty."

He looked up from what he was doing. Looked at her more closely. "That soft red sweater suits you," he said mildly. "You look good."

She waited, her heart thudding. Waited for more. Waited for him to step in her direction.

He didn't. He simply looked down again, went on measuring, then marking, different boards.

"Why should you feel guilty, Alice? Did it ever cross your mind that I like doing this? That I'm actually having fun? I haven't done anything like this for years, not since my student days when I spent a whole summer helping a friend restore a rotten Victorian wreck of a house. Now I realize how much I've missed using my hands to construct something, do something positive and physical such as saving this building from further degradation."

She had to be satisfied with the answer. Either that or stand here gaping at him and wringing her hands, feeling perfectly foolish. And lusting after the man. Wishing that one of them would dare make the first move toward some intimacy.

****

"Attractive new habit you've picked up. Exactly what every elegant woman needs." Rose Badger winced. "Alice, sweetie, since when have you been a nail-biter? Refusing to wear nail polish is one thing, but destroying your look is another neurosis altogether."

Alice, sitting with Rose in the back room of her shop, jumped in her seat. She hadn't been aware that she'd been chewing on her thumb. She looked down, contemplated the damage. "I don't suppose that one half-eaten nail is going to dramatically change my so-called 'look' very much."

Rose raised the huge bowl full of mashed avocado she was mixing. "Perhaps an avocado face mask would work wonders?"

"Is that what you're planning to do with that mess?"

"Mess? I'll have you know this is a one hundred percent true beauty bomb. Tracey Kipps is taking me dancing tonight."

"Tracey Kipps?" Alice raised her eyebrows, momentarily intrigued. "Is Tracey in the picture again? I thought you'd pretty well run him out of town with a double-barreled lipstick tube a year or two ago."

"Alice, dear," said Rose, infinite patience in her voice. "This is the civilized state of Nevada, not the Wild West. Actually—" She winked. "It doesn't do a man any harm to show him he's not indispensable. As far as I can guess, no woman ever rejected Tracey before. If they had, he'd have learned how to behave long ago."

"So it's working this time around?" asked Alice.

"Working? With Tracey?" Rose paused, looked uncertain, secretive. Then smiled coquettishly. "Tracey's not the main man on my horizon, but I'm letting myself be spoiled rotten by him—the promise of a luxurious holiday together, a big box of dark chocolate, the works."

Alice wasn't fooled. Her friend was hiding something. What? But if Rose wasn't forthcoming, she didn't have the right to probe. She had too many secrets of her own. "Dark chocolate in Blake's Folly? I am impressed."

Rose frowned. "Dark chocolate or not, I'm keeping my options wide open."

"And keeping your stable of admirers on tenterhooks. How do you manage it?"

"To tell the truth, a holiday alone with Tracey does sound suffocating, no matter how glamorous or exotic the setting."

"Okay. I'll buy that. Especially if Tracey isn't the main man."

"Right."

Alice waited, but Rose remained silent. The temptation to pry was irresistible. "Come on. Tell me what's going on. Have you met someone more intriguing than Tracey, or Lance, or Mike, or Roy, or Jim, or Bernie?"

Rose bit her lip. Forbidding herself to reveal anything? Then, sighing deeply, she capitulated. "Okay. Intriguing, yes. There's Jonah—Jonah Livingstone. He's not a potential lover; he's not a potential admirer, okay? Just a very engaging person, a geologist, and he makes my other men seem a little dull." Then her eyes narrowed. "But why in heaven's name are we talking about me? You're the one with the interesting life at the moment. How are things going with that sexy, passionate lodger of yours?"

"Passionate? Don't let your imagination run away with you." Alice hunched back in her seat. She hated talking about this. But she felt so uncertain about her feelings, about everything in her life, she had to talk to someone, and she certainly couldn't bring up the subject with Jace.

"Alice? You walked into my workroom, sat down, and didn't say one word for over half an hour. Whenever I asked you a question, you looked blank, as if you were a thousand miles away. That's not normal behavior, not even for you. What's going on?"

"Nothing's going on. Really. Why are you grilling me like this?"

"Romance with Jace is giving you problems?" Rose rolled her eyes. "Of course it is. Why ask?"

"Oh, honestly, Rose. Do you always have to dream up romances? Not everyone thinks the same way you do, you know!"

Rose began stirring the avocado mash as if Alice had said nothing at all.

"Oh, I'm sorry." Alice reached out and touched her

friend's hand apologetically. "I don't mean to be so touchy. It's…"

"It's what?"

Alice sighed. "Look, I've been independent Alice Treemont for years now, okay?"

"Okay. So?"

"This is hard for me to admit. I don't know how to put it. Let's say it's difficult for me to confide in you."

"Could have fooled me," muttered Rose sarcastically.

"Not because I don't trust you, but because I never tell anyone what I'm feeling. And now, here I am, confused as hell. I don't know what's happening to me. As far as Jace is concerned, I mean." She raised her hands in a vague, meaningless gesture. "I guess you could say I've got a terrible crush on him. Like a teenager. Except I'm no teen." She stopped, looked at Rose beseechingly. "Listen to how infantile this girlie conversation is. Let's change the subject, okay?"

Rose ignored the plea. "I don't believe you. It's no crush."

"No? All right. No crush. A crush sounds silly. I admit everything. I want him. I can't stop thinking about him. I can't think about anything else, and that's undignified and ridiculous. For an adult, anyway. I hate being like this."

"Emotion is emotion. Caring about someone, wanting someone has nothing to do with age or being an adult."

"That's what one part of my brain keeps saying to the other, but the other side doesn't agree."

Rose's lips curled into a faintly mocking curve. "And what does the other side say?"

"That this is all one-sided. That nothing intimate is going on. How could there be? There's Tanya."

"Who's Tanya?"

"His woman back in Chicago. With a name like Tanya, I'm getting all sorts of seductive images."

"Tanya from Chicago doesn't sound good, I'll admit that." Rose's face had taken on a pensive expression.

"You see?"

"Almost. How does Jace feel about you?"

Alice looked at Rose as though she'd begun swinging from the overhead light. "How am I supposed to know that?"

"Take a wild guess."

"I wouldn't dare."

"Ma Handy has been telling everyone that Jace couldn't keep his eyes off you the whole time you sat in that tacky living room of hers!"

"The cow! She didn't!" Alice stopped and then stared. "He couldn't?"

Rose nodded sagely. "So Ma says. And Alice, if you don't want Ma gossiping about you, she's the last person you should go calling on."

"It was Jace's fault. He wanted to buy some wood from Pa to fix my house up."

Rose slathered a gluey mess of avocado mash across her forehead. "I heard about that, too. Everyone in town has been talking about the way he's propping up that ruin of yours."

"Lord help me! Isn't that typical. Jace started doing it one day ago!"

"News travels fast over two square miles, most of them uninhabited. And I must say, the news sounds good to me."

"Fixing up a house? Any good friend would do that."

Rose continued slathering, and her naturally creamy complexion disappeared completely under the thick greenish slime. "Oh, you think so, do you? Stop dreaming. And stop worrying."

"Advise me to stop breathing," Alice said, her voice grim. She sank back into the large armchair again. "Here's how things look. I think it's possible that I've fallen madly in love, but the person I'm in love with really sees me as a screwy old dame who lives in the desert and spends her time spying on snakes."

The area that must have been Rose's mouth twitched. "Not an unreasonable description. But I don't know what the problem is."

"Who'd want to stick around a screwy old dame? Especially when there's a gorgeous Tanya somewhere in the background?"

"Why don't you live for the moment? Enjoy life, enjoy Jace, and enjoy what you have together. Besides, you're no fortune-teller. You don't know what the future will bring."

Alice stared at her green-smeared friend. "You look awful. I feel like I'm talking to a plant."

"Why worry? It's more rewarding talking to plants than to most of the folks around here. Besides, my name is Rose. So tell me, why are you chewing at your thumbnail again?"

Alice groaned. "You don't know what else I've done."

"Now I'm starting to feel slightly ill. Go on…"

"Well, everything was going along fine. Jace went so far as to defend snakes the other night when a horrible creep threatened me."

"Poor, doomed man."

"And then I went and ruined everything." She hunched forward. "I told him that there was someone else in my life."

"You did what?"

"Brad. I said that Brad Mace and I…" Alice was too miserable to finish the sentence.

"What did you do a stupid thing like that for?"

"I was scared. There was that Tanya in the picture and all the upheaval to contend with. I mean, look what Jace has done to my life. I was perfectly happy before he flashed into town and turned everything upside down. I had to defend myself. And now…well…I don't want to do that anymore. But if I admit the truth about Brad, Jace will think I'm racing after him and desperate. And a liar. Bad image. So now it's too late."

Two blue eyes, caught in the verdant goo, looked pensive. "Maybe not."

"Meaning?"

"Nothing is hopeless, Alice. Why don't we think up a plan? Let's call it the Tactic. You panicked; you chased him off. Now put the Tactic into action."

"Which means what?"

"The Tactic means making a wild play for Jace. Show him he matters, that he fits into your life. See what happens."

"He'll probably go back to Tanya when he's through with me," said Alice grimly.

"Most likely. Only crazy people choose to live permanently in semi-ghost towns. But, at the very least, you'll have had a wonderful affair. Besides, Chicago is still in the United States, last time I heard. How do you know he won't ask you to come and visit? You don't need a passport. And these days, you can get on a plane and fly all the way there, nonstop."

"You're incorrigible." Alice got to her feet.

"Hey, Alice? Before you go, let me give you a tip. Why don't you act sort of normal-feminine for a while? You know what I mean."

"I am. I'm cooking something wonderful for lunch—a sambal made with coconut milk, red peppers, onions. Something to show how grateful I am that he's repairing the things I always meant to get around to fixing but never managed to find the time to do them in, or because I couldn't afford the supplies."

"Cooking another meal is not quite what I had in mind. Stop being so domestic, and do something more direct. Think Tactic, and that means big-time signaling. Go for lipstick, eyeliner, low-cut sweaters, sultry looks, and touching. You know the stuff—your fingers resting on his arm for longer than they should, your hips brushing against his in the hallway."

"Sure. That's my scene. Transparent negligees, toeless shoes with rhinestones, ostrich-feather boas. Blake's Folly brothel at its best." Alice chewed back a giggle. She knew, deep inside, those things wouldn't attract Jace. He'd probably seen it all back in Chicago. She couldn't pretend to be what she wasn't either; he'd see through the game. Instinct was telling her that he actually liked her for the person she was.

"Well, if you're not willing to try all the standard tricks of the trade, perhaps you could start acting frail, more helpless, and less independent. You know what I mean: stereotype female. That might excite him, bring out his protective male instinct." Rose stopped, cocked her green head to one side, and a mischievous white-toothed grin appeared. "Oh, forget it. It's far too late to claim that rattlesnakes scare you, so it will be useless if you pretend to faint when you see a spider."

Chapter Ten

Hibernaculum

"Alice, that was an incredible meal!" Jace sighed with satisfaction as he put down his fork.

"I aim to please," said Alice calmly. But she was delighted. Very much so. "I do want to show you how much I appreciate the work you're doing on the house."

Jace looked at her. She'd come a long way toward trusting him too. Was she aware of that? That's what one of the goals of the Charm Plan had been. Now it was time for the second step—as much as he disliked the idea of part two of the Plan. It was called "sharing interests." Now or never. "There is something else I want from you, Alice."

"Oh?" She didn't look wary anymore. Dreamy perhaps. He'd have given anything to be able to read her mind.

"Sure. I'd like you to teach me a few things."

"Teach?" She waited.

"Yeah." Jace hesitated. Then battled on despite the squeamishness in his gut. "About snakes."

"Snakes?" She stared as if hearing the word for the first time in her life.

"That's right."

"Why?"

"Why not?" It was pure bluff on his part. He could

think of about twenty thousand reasons why not. To start with, the idea made his skin crawl and his throat close with fear. But he'd learn about snakes even if he died in the attempt—which seemed a definite possibility—and Alice would learn how nice it could be to do things together instead of retreating into her own world, instead of locking him out. She'd see that, if they didn't have a lot in common at the moment, a relationship could grow and interests could be shared.

Did he dare look deeply into why he wanted those things? Did he know? Yes, he desired Alice, but that wasn't all. She touched him inside, and he'd never felt like this before. Perhaps he was teaching himself what the word trust could really mean.

Conflicting emotions chased each other across her face. "If that's what you really want," she said finally. She didn't sound as though she believed him. Not really. No, she was gaping at him as if he'd lost his mind.

Which he probably had. "Lesson one right now, okay?"

"Okay. Go get your jacket. I'll take you to a hibernaculum—a hibernation hole."

****

As they trudged back out into the dull rocky wasteland, Jace tried to squash the queasy sensations that started high in his throat and continued on down until they reached the tips of his toes. He was reacting like a weakling, and he hated himself for it, but if Alice couldn't read the expression on his face, then he might get through this experience with a little dignity. Perhaps the best thing to do was make a little easy conversation—although all his thoughts were turning around snakes at the moment.

"Do you actually have a degree in herpetology?"

"There isn't one. You can have a degree in biology or zoology but not in herpetology. Actually, quite a few of the people doing high-quality research in herpetology are self-taught. One of the most famous is a salesman in Texas."

"Interesting," said Jace and hated himself for sounding so faint.

"You sure you're all right with this?" Alice reached out, touched his arm gently. There was no condescension in her voice.

"Keep touching me, and I will be," he joked, trying to seem light-hearted. Not that it wasn't the truth. He loved it when they touched.

He saw her eyes flicker, wondered what that meant. Not "no." Definitely not a rejection, instinct said. Every passing minute told him that the Plan was working its magic. She was showing tenderness, and he liked being the object of it. Basked in it. Nothing was more satisfying than to see a strong independent woman begin to melt.

"Jace, whenever you do see a snake, try and appreciate the creature. See the beauty of its movements, its markings. Find aesthetic appreciation."

"Sure." He tried not to shiver. Could he really get over his repulsion? He doubted it.

"Think also that the snake is a victim, not an aggressor."

"Right. That should be easy: a five-foot-long slithering victim with deadly poison." But he told himself to relax, to think about how good it felt out here. Because that, at least, was true. Straggling tufts of vegetation, tickled by a chilly breeze, shimmered along the broad horizon. And the silence? Well, he'd already gotten used to that, too. Life without the noise of traffic and big city clatter did have appeal. "Okay. Reassure me. Tell me more about snakes being victims."

"Okay. Well, for one, so many are killed by cars because they love to go bask in the heat on the road. And if most people are instinctively afraid of snakes, snakes aren't instinctively afraid of people, so they sometimes slide into backyards, innocently passing through on their way to somewhere else. They should be left alone, of course, but people kill them as soon as they notice them. Then, there's the danger of habitat destruction."

"And rattlesnake roundups," he added, to his own surprise.

Her eyes flickered. "That's right. Very few snakes manage to survive their first encounter with man. But snakes have other enemies, too. Hawks, owls, coyotes, roadrunners, bobcats, skunks, badgers, and other snakes all prey on newborn rattlers."

Jace nodded and wisely kept any further comment to himself, although he couldn't help feeling the coyotes and bobcats were on his side. But he couldn't allow himself to think that way. Not now. He had to concentrate on following Alice out into the back of beyond, his steps matching hers, their hands brushing from time to time.

"Everyone should remember how important snakes are," Alice continued. "They eat animals most people want to get rid of—mice, shrews, rats, moles, gophers, lizards, rabbits, and other snakes. Carrion, too." She stopped suddenly, pointed to the ground a short distance away, to a crack under a scattering of rocks. "See that crevice?"

He did. It was a long, innocuous-looking fissure,

nothing more.

"Well, that's one of the best hibernation places I know. What's really interesting is that, although snakes are loners, they meet up with other snakes to hibernate. The babies follow their mother's scent, and some of these hibernacula have been used for centuries. Inside, you can find hundreds of snakes as well as the other creatures they share the space with. Tortoises, for example."

"Hundreds of snakes in that one hole," Jace said thoughtfully.

"We won't see them now, of course. It's too cold. They won't come out until the spring, and you probably won't be here then."

Her expression hadn't changed, nor had her voice. He must have imagined the faint note of wistfulness. Spring in the desert, she'd said? It didn't sound half bad. But Chicago was waiting for him. The publishing work he did at the university was waiting. He couldn't stay out here forever.

Alice must have misinterpreted his silence. "Having second thoughts about learning more?"

"No," he said honestly. "Trying to educate myself, although I've got a long way to go. All those snakes curled up almost under our feet sounds treacherous and very unpleasant."

"I imagine it does to most people. Which is why I want to share my appreciation and knowledge of them with everyone by photographing them, writing about them."

"A fearless woman," he teased.

Her pale eyes met his soberly. "No. I'd never say that. I'd be lying if I did."

"Okay. But a very original, independent one, though."

The toe of her walking boot scratched the surface of the prairie floor. "I was a very different person when I was younger. I had to spend years building up independence. Having done that, it's become hard for me to show vulnerability."

Amazing, she'd actually admitted it. Jace could hardly believe his ears. But he knew he couldn't react. She'd probably clam up again if he did. Instead, he said, as smoothly as possible and without the slightest trace of a grin, "That must make things very difficult in your relationship."

Alice's head snapped up. "Relationship?" she said faintly.

"With Brad. You know. The rancher."

"Oh. Oh, yes. Brad." She managed a smile, a forced one, perfectly false.

"The all-Western he-man." Jace nodded. He knew he couldn't question her further on this particular subject. Not now. But he had a very definite feeling there really was no threatening Brad in the picture. Of course there wasn't. She'd invented a love story with Brad because she'd needed to put some distance between them. Now all he had to do was be patient. Live for the moment. Stay cool. He glanced back at the crevice in the ground, not more than twenty feet away.

Alice followed his eyes. "How does it feel to be so close to the creatures you hate so much?"

"Hate? Do I really hate them? I wonder. I have a phobia, that's the problem. But why hang onto a phobia when there's a chance of getting rid of it and making your life happier? No, I'll get used to those creatures, I'm sure I will. Sometimes we need to get familiar with the idea of things before we can really accept them and care for them."

"I suppose so," Alice said softly.

He wondered if they were both referring to reptiles.

Chapter Eleven

In the Attic

"You bringing Jace to the Get-Together tomorrow evening?" Sitting at the long brown table in Alice's kitchen, Rose examined her reflection on the back of a teaspoon.

"To the Blake's Folly Annual Get-Together at the Mizpah Saloon?" Alice stared at her friend. "Are you crazy?"

"Not yet. But I'm working on it." She put down the spoon. "So why aren't you inviting him? You might both have fun."

"No way." Alice would fight this new idea of Rose's tooth and nail. "Go there with Jace? He'd hate every minute of it!"

"How do you know he'd hate it?"

"You know the answer as well as I do. Sly Grimes is going to sing, and he's terrible. And the Old Boy's Band is about as awful as you can get."

Rose's nose wrinkled. "Awful isn't the word. Try gruesome. Painful." She reached for her purse, dug around, pulled out a tube of pearly lipstick. "But that isn't important. What matters is asking him to go someplace with you. That's a perfect Tactic maneuver."

"Tactic maneuver or not, I can't ask Jace to the Get-Together. He'd never forgive me."

"So what does he expect out here in the desert? Mozart? Beethoven? Shostakovich? Slavic melodies?"

"Well, I suppose it doesn't matter since I'm not going to ask him anyway."

"Of course you're not. You're too much of a crank to do something simple like asking Jace to a normal country dance in your own normal community."

"Don't fool yourself. Blake's Folly is not normal. Think how everyone will stare. At me. At Jace. It'll be about as much fun as being on display in a cage at the zoo."

"Yeah. I know." Rose screwed the lipstick back down into its tube. "When I told Jane Grimes I was coming over here for coffee this morning, she said this whole community was waiting to see the two of you together. She said that Mick Fletcher told Tony that Lucy Miller spent all her time blabbing about you. She says the reason nobody ever sees the two of you is because you and Jace spend all your time holed up here. In bed. That you're both living out a deep, intense, obsessive sexual passion." Rose stood, reached for her coat. "So I guess it's up to you. You want to make a public appearance or keep all those rumors flying?"

****

It had been years since she'd dumped all these boxes and bags in the attic. How many times had she thought of coming up here, sorting everything out, and giving it away? At least a million. Then she hadn't done that after all.

Alice, sitting on the floor in the midst of the chaos, clicked open the catch of yet another expensive beige suitcase. On top was the black sheath dress she'd bought so long ago. Elegant and chic, it would never go out of style. The same with the brightly colored silk blouses, skirts. Stylish things. Classics. But out here, in this life, they weren't classics; they were leftovers from a painful past. Items so charged with bitter memories, she had vowed never to wear—or touch—them again in case they were cursed and had the power to destroy everything positive.

The faint odor of some forgotten perfume rose in the still air. It all seemed so long ago. It *was* so long ago. Another lifetime. When she'd been another woman.

Take this red bit of froth. She'd worn it once, and she could remember the night. The party, noisy and crowded, with the cream of Hollywood society. There had been a well-known rock group and a large yellow-and-green-striped tent. She hadn't wanted to be there. Her face ached from smiling, from trying to look happy when she was miserable; her eyes burned from the effort of staying wide open and alert-looking. And all she'd wanted was to be alone, far away from the intolerable noise, the banal chitchat.

"Where's H.B.?" someone near her had asked.

"On location," she'd answered. Made the usual effort at keeping all emotion out of her voice. That's what was expected of her. The paparazzi, the gossip columnists, the society vultures, the people who pretended to be your friends would swoop down and gobble you up if they saw the slightest crack in your armor.

In reality, she'd had no idea where H.B. was. He'd been on location…last week. This week, she hadn't been able to reach him. He was in some location, all right. Holed up with his latest leading lady. Or someone else. Or a whole harem of willing ladies. It didn't matter. One cluster of groupies this week, next week, another. Many marriages were like that in their circle: one partner running his or her show, leaving the other to steer a rudderless boat through treacherous water.

Why had she gone to that party? Why go to all those social events she hated? Because she had to be seen with people who were important, had to keep up the image of the happy wife of a powerful man. Doing the job H.B. demanded of her, that her acting career required. If you were invited, then it meant you were at the top and doing okay. Because no one invited a loser. That's how you gauged your position.

"Alice?"

A voice jerked her out of the past and back into now. Jace's voice. He was home! Her heart soared.

"Alice, where are you?"

He would come upstairs looking for her, see the attic door was open. She glanced at all the heaped pretty fabrics, the soft colors. No time to stuff all these things back into suitcases. Besides, why bother? She was this Alice now, not that other one.

"Jace? I'm up in the attic."

The last rays of afternoon sun lit the minuscule particles of dust floating lazily in the calm air. And here was Jace now, standing in the doorway, staring at her. Not at the mess spread all around her. Was that happiness in his wonderful green eyes? Happiness at seeing her? Her heart swelled.

Then his expression changed to puzzlement. Slowly, he entered the attic space, sat down on an overturned wooden packing case.

"How was your day?" She was going to sound casual if it killed her.

He didn't bother answering. Instead, he gestured to the clothes, the many open suitcases. "What's all of this?"

"The remains of my former life," Alice said, her voice dry. "The frills. Or, to be more precise, what's left of the frills. It's the first time I've dared open up the cases. I was afraid…"

"Afraid?"

"I thought it might be like opening Pandora's box."

His expression was unreadable. "What former life?"

"My days in Hollywood. When I was Alice Bates, the actress married to H.B. Bates."

"Bates? The film mogul?"

"That's the one."

"Oh. Funny…I've been wondering about your former life ever since I met you, but I never imagined you as an actress."

"It wasn't a brilliant career. Four films, one of them never released. Some television, which I hated. Quite a lot of live theater, which I really loved, and which H.B. hated. He wanted his wife to be on the big screen, to be seen by millions. It upped his status."

"It's a big jump from Hollywood to Blake's Folly." He didn't look impressed by her past. He didn't look astonished either, Alice noted. Just curious. Which was a relief. It made things easier for her.

"The only jump I felt that I could take," she said calmly. "Because I chickened out. Got cold feet. All those sloshing turquoise swimming pools were making me seasick, and I was woozy from living a life where everyone talked obsessively about the tranquilizers they needed to stay calm during the day, the sleeping pills they conked out with at night. Then there was the ocean of booze and, last but not least, the revolving friends."

"Revolving friends?"

"People you make a point of knowing because they write the most successful sitcoms. Then, when the sitcom flops, when it doesn't make it to the next season, you can't see them anymore. No way you're going to be caught dead lying around their heart-shaped swimming pool, cocktail in hand, in case someone sees you and thinks you're on a losing streak too. Those were the rules. H.B. insisted on that."

"How did you link up with H.B.?"

"I met him when a friend, Cindy, dragged me to a party. She was an aspiring actress, determined to make important contacts and break into the big time. I was a student, finishing my degree in zoology. H.B. happened to be there. He saw me, liked my looks, and decided he wanted me in his stable."

"And you? How did you feel?"

"I was young, I was naive. He overwhelmed me. I hadn't had much of a childhood, and certainly no fun and no glamour. My mother ran away from Blake's Folly because she was pregnant with me—apparently my father was married to someone else, and she never told me who he was. We lived in Sacramento while I was growing up, then we ended up in L.A., where her lover of the moment got her into doing peep shows. When that relationship ended, we lived on welfare until she managed to find other guys—losers, usually—to pick up the tab. Then she died."

"But you managed to get through college?"

"The first doctorate in the family," she said proudly. "Science always fascinated me, and before getting married, I worked as a waitress, then got modeling jobs so I could have the money to study and get a degree. I've been fascinated by reptiles ever since childhood, and I'd dreamed of being a herpetologist. Of course, H.B. had other plans for me."

"Were you happy with him? Ever?"

"Dazzled at first, but it wasn't much of a marriage. We didn't trust each other. Nobody trusted anyone in our circle. No one had a real conversation other than mentioning the new sauna with piped-in music, the latest fad therapy group, the trendiest restaurant, the laziness of hired help. Life seemed to be nothing more than one big, very banal consumer party. Right from the beginning, H.B. went from one infidelity to another. I was expected to do the same. Fun and games. H.B. suggested I go into therapy to adjust. Squeeze into the right shape for that empty, sad life."

"You don't miss acting?"

"Miss it? Never. That life happened to someone else. I wonder how I tolerated it for so long. In the end, I thought I'd go crazy if I didn't start doing something that had meaning for me."

"So you came out here, to the desert?"

"Not right away." The old memories welled up again. The horror of the last days of her marriage. "Something awful had to happen first, and I'm sure you heard about it."

"Doesn't ring a bell. Remind me."

"H.B. went away for a wild orgy weekend with a group of like-minded friends and his latest heartthrob. There was an accident. One of the girls drowned. She was a week away from her sixteenth birthday."

Jace nodded slowly. "Ah, yes, I remember reading something about that. Vaguely. There were drugs involved, weren't there? Wasn't H.B. arrested?"

"Temporarily. In the scandal that followed, I couldn't make a move without a horde of photographers following me. Every little detail of our life was taken up by the scandal press. It was humiliating." Alice stopped, looked away.

Jace was watching her closely. "Is there more to the story?" he asked gently.

"There is. But I've never talked about it." She didn't want to talk about it now either, although she knew she had to. She wanted to confide in Jace, to stop keeping everything secret. She took a deep breath. "There was a baby. My little girl. She was premature. She tried to hold on for as long as she could, but she didn't survive." The grief was still strong, perhaps because she'd kept silent for so long.

"How did H.B. react to that?"

Alice remembered her despair, her helplessness. "When H.B. first found out I was pregnant, he was furious. I wanted a child, but he never did. He refused to believe he was the baby's father. He was so certain I lived by the same moral code he did. That I was like my mother." Knuckles white, her fingers twisted a pale silk ribbon. "He was relieved, even pleased, when our baby died."

"And then?"

She pushed away the old feeling of sorrow, replaced it with one of pride. "I finally stood up for myself and for what I wanted. Finally. I left H.B., left our flashy home, our big cars, and the life that had been making me miserable for so long. I came out here, to this house my grandfather had left me, joined the herpetological society in Reno, and began reading everything I could about snakes. When I became knowledgeable enough, I started working as a herpetologist."

"And H.B.?"

"He left the country for a while. Came back after he managed to lie his way out of the scandal and pay a huge lump sum to the dead girl's family. He then went on to more suitable wives. I think he's had two or three since me. I've managed to stay away from him. He doesn't know where I am, and I've never asked for a penny from him."

Jace's brow wrinkled in puzzlement. "Why have you always avoided talking about this? Every time I asked you a personal question, you made me feel like I was prying into a deep, dark secret."

She couldn't help her rueful smile. "Because my past is a deep, dark secret. For me, it is. I don't want to be associated with that old life and all the unhappiness. I'm not that other Alice, that brainless, beautiful Alice of the past. I'm this one. Also, I didn't want you identifying me with H.B. He's so famous, and the story was so sordid, so humiliating."

"And you thought something like that would matter to me?"

"I didn't know you," she said defensively. She knew better now, of course. Or she thought she did. Dropping the shred of ribbon, she reached behind, grabbed a large, black photo album. Handed it to him. "Take a look at the other Alice."

He opened it. There she was, young Alice, with shimmering blonde hair tumbling over her shoulders. A perfect Hollywood beauty, the sort of woman who'd once attracted the powerful H.B. Bates. He pointed to another photo. "How old were you here?"

143

J. Arlene Culiner

Dressed in a skimpy bikini, the former Alice stood by a pink swimming pool, cocktail in hand, laughing into the camera lens. "Around twenty-five." What else could she add? Jace probably preferred that other woman. "I was pretty then," she added. It wasn't a question.

"I like the way you are now."

"Oh, come on, Jace!"

He closed the album. Frowned. "What are you trying to do? Convince me I don't know what I like? I prefer the older Alice, the one you are now. Alice with laugh lines, with the wisdom that life brings. The Alice I'm getting to know. Desert Alice. Snake-lady Alice. Alice who's sitting right in front of me. That other Alice, the young Hollywood version, was beautiful and glamorous. But I don't know her."

She stared down at the floor, touched. "Well, it's mighty nice of you to say that." She suddenly felt so shy.

"I'm not saying it to be nice."

"That's nice too." She sounded ridiculous. Like a foolish four-year-old. She started laughing. Jace's laughter joined hers. Tension shattered into a million pieces.

"I'd almost forgotten why I came up to the attic in the first place," she said when she finally found her voice again. "It's because I've decided to stop hiding from my past. Clothes are no more than sewn-together pieces of fabric. They aren't jinxed; they can't suddenly come alive and drag me back in time. So I've let myself remember how nice some of these are. You see...I wanted to find something normal to wear."

His eyes glinted. "Normal?"

"Normal." She nodded. "Totally normal and perfectly feminine—according to Rose Badger's idea of

144

womanhood, that is. Because I was going to ask you out."

"You were?" He looked very chuffed.

"Now, don't start getting all excited." She grimaced before continuing. "I'm inviting you to the Blake's Folly Get-Together tomorrow night."

He was still looking chuffed. "Fine with me!"

"Don't you want me to tell you what it is?" She doubted he'd look so happy when he knew.

"I don't care what it is."

"You'll be sorry," she said ominously. "Does that mean you'll accept the invitation?"

Jace's smile suddenly vanished, and he looked at her soberly. "There is one major problem. I don't know if I really ought to accept."

"Oh." Why did she feel so damned disappointed? "Why not? Or shouldn't I ask?" But seeing the glint in his eyes, she realized he was about to tease her. Again.

"What's Brad going to say?" Jace asked. "About you asking me out?"

"Oh. Oh, yes. Brad." Hell. How was she going to get out of this one? What could she say without looking completely ridiculous?

"I mean, Brad is the important man in your life," Jace continued, his face poker straight. "Shouldn't you be going to the Get-Together with him?"

Alice sniffed. "Oh, don't you worry about Brad." She waved her left hand, a theatrical gesture of dismissal. "Poor Brad's got his hands full out at that ranch of his. No time for fun and games with a whole herd of chickens to milk."

Jace's burst of laughter permitted them to drop the thorny subject.

Chapter Twelve

The Get-Together

Alice sat on the sagging settee on the veranda, waiting for Jace to get ready. And thinking about how the water in the shower was running over his glorious body at this very moment.

Back down, Alice. Think about something cool and calming. She tried. Thoughts about cold nights made her think about how a naked Jace in her bed would warm those nights up very nicely. Forcing herself to concentrate on rattlesnakes had her thinking about the coiling and slithering movements she'd like to be performing on Jace's body. Thoughts about the dogs led to ideas about how soft their fur was and what it would feel like to touch that rough curl of hair on Jace's chest. Hell. If she didn't manage to get some semblance of discipline into her thoughts, there was no way she'd be able to hold up her end of a normal conversation tonight.

She didn't know if her feelings bordered more on relief or plain lust when he finally appeared in front of her, wet hair curled back into a temporary order, hard muscular legs encased in fresh jeans that did nothing to hide the slenderness of his hips. His dark turtleneck sweater reminded her how tight his belly was.

His eyes were caressing her slowly too. Warmly, probingly. Taking in the silk blouse that softened her frame under the loose open jacket, the billowing skirt that emphasized her narrow waist.

"Ready?" He held his hand out with a smile.

Ready? Oh boy, she was ready, all right. He laced her fingers through his. It certainly was anything but normal to feel the sweet, bright electricity jolt through her as they touched. We're holding hands, that's all, she chided herself. Calm down. She couldn't. Her knees felt like damp sponge cake; her head was a high-flying balloon attached by a gossamer thread. Desire, anticipation—these things could make you crazy.

He must have felt the tension as it zinged its way around her body. "Is everything okay?"

"Fine. Great!" She wished he would be less polite. That he suddenly felt the urge to maul her. No, turn that one around. She wished that she had the courage to be less ladylike and polite. That she could find the nerve to start mauling him.

They crossed through Blake's Folly on foot, and for once, she didn't notice, or care, how many window curtains twitched as nosy eyes marked their passage. She was proud to be seen walking with Jace. What had changed? She had. She'd finally allowed herself to feel, to be alive. To care. To want.

The Mizpah Saloon loomed in front of them. Square, bulky, built in the 1870s, it had once been considered a den of perdition where bouts of gambling, wild drinking, and womanizing usually ended in deadly shootouts. And whenever a volley of shots had rung out, residents ducked, held their breath, waited for the final shot signaling the coup de grâce.

Times had certainly changed. In the upstairs bedrooms, sagging beds and odd sticks of furniture sat undisturbed under thick pale layers of dust. Only the grand downstairs barroom was in use, its high ceiling and cornices the pride of all Blake's Folly. Tonight, that room was overheated and filled with people.

The so-called music hit Alice and Jace with force as they pushed open the wide front door. The Old Boy's Band was in full swing, with Sly Grimes attacking a badly tuned guitar, Pa Handy torturing an accordion, Tony Ripe poking at a fiddle, Luke Miller violently slapping a piano, and Bill Flats bashing away at something that had, once upon a time, been a snare drum. The resulting noise resembled, with a great deal of imagination, the "Tennessee Waltz." It hurled itself around the room aggressively.

No, not hurled, thought Alice. Thudded or stomped. She observed Jace out of the corner of her eye. He looked neither terrified, nor horrified, nor disgusted. He looked…amused?

"Uh, Jace," she began.

"So this is the famous Get-Together?" A grin tugged the corners of his mouth.

"It's the social event of the year," she said rather apologetically. "You think you're going to survive this?"

"I think I'm going to enjoy it."

He had to be joking. She, Alice, could enjoy this. She lived here. This was her community; these people were her friends—despite the fact that they were often nosy and interfering. But Jace couldn't feel the same way. That was impossible.

Jace helped her off with her jacket and handed it to a strange-looking Mary-Jane Lothar, who had got herself up like a badly dressed hatcheck girl from a gangster film of the thirties. Alice tried not to stare. Things were getting worse and worse, and she was certain they weren't about to stop, but it would help if she could stop agonizing.

The music slid to a wheezing halt, and Sly Grimes, dressed in a cowboy shirt complete with fringes, tight suede trousers, and red boots with colored spurs, grabbed a microphone.

"Well, folks, it's mah-tty fine seeing yawl heah." Sly Grimes, born and bred in Blake's Folly, seemed to have acquired a deep and very odd southern drawl: his long-standing ambition to be a famous but local country singer stopped at nothing.

"For this verah special occasion, I've written this he-ah song of mine, and I'm sure it'll be something you c'n all appreciate. I'm hoping it'll reach the top of the chee-arts soon." Sly Grimes never did claim to be modest. "Song's called 'Gonna Love You Till I Die.' "

He turned to the musicians with the glittery smile of a television star. "Okay, boys. Let it roll!"

Roll was certainly a wild exaggeration. The band began trudging its way through a dreary sort of dirge. Alice, full of misgivings, flinched. Damn Rose and her silly ideas.

"I'm gonna love you till I die,
And that, baby, ain't no lie.
Comin' home, comin' home,
To-oo you-oo..."

"Uh, Jace? Look, Sly Grimes isn't exactly a top-notch pro."

"No, he isn't," Jace confirmed as Sly attempted a high note and failed, utterly, to approach it. However, as if to show that where there's a will there's a way, a few couples made their way onto the dance floor and began to shuffle around, searching for a beat. Two of the dancers were Rose Badger and a man Alice had never seen before. Could this be the geologist Rose had alluded to? The mysterious Jonah Livingstone? If so, he was looking down at Rose as if he'd reached Nirvana.

"Nice to see you here." Jane Grimes, Sly's proud mother, tapped her heartily on the shoulder. She was dressed to the hilt—as befitted a parent of the Star of the evening—in a bizarre concoction of floppy pink net. Jane stared unabashedly at Jace. "This here your new lodger?" The very special emphasis on the word "lodger" made her meaning unmistakable.

"Yes," answered Alice coolly. "My lodger, Jace Constant. And he's from Chicago, and he's a writer, a historian, and yes, he's been fixing up my house." Might as well make sure local gossip got all the facts right and in the proper order, she thought defiantly.

"Hear you went to Lucy's for a meal out," said Jane with a grin of satisfaction.

Alice almost hissed with exasperation. "How on earth did you know about that? Really, this town is too much!"

"Tony's uncle Greg happened to be out that way and saw you both go in there."

"And, of course, he reported in as soon as possible," responded Alice darkly. Now she dared steal a look at Jace. The corners of his mouth were twitching madly, as if he were making a supreme effort to repress a grin.

What was there to grin about, Alice wondered morosely. She could imagine Jace describing this social event to a group of sneering Chicago sophisticates. She could hear their chortling now. This had been a mistake, a really terrible mistake. Perhaps if she got him out of here as quickly as possible, she could reduce the damage.

"Listen, Jace, we can leave if you want. You must think this is awful. I mean, compared to what you must get up to in Chicago…"

"Forget Chicago. Comparing Blake's Folly to Chicago is like comparing an earthworm to a rattler."

"What's that supposed to mean?" she asked, feeling defensive.

"Nothing to get offended about," Jace said, a mysterious half grin playing over his wonderful mouth. "Earthworms and rattlers are very nice and useful creatures. Would you care to dance?" The change of subject was too abrupt for Alice to be able to muster up any biting answer. And now that Jace's fingers were closing over hers, now that he was pulling her smoothly into his arms, biting answers had absolutely no chance whatsoever.

Dancing with Jace. Well, wasn't this something. Her heart was thundering wildly in her ears, and all her attention was focused on his arms tightening around her, molding her body to his own without once losing step to the music—such as it was. Enveloped in his warmth, surrounded by the wonderful male scent of him…it was lovely. As if sensing how she felt, he pulled her closer. Closing her eyes, she rested her head on his shoulder and let her body soften. Succumb. His warm breath fluttered over the top of her hair.

It was heavenly. Even better, it was pure paradise. The words rolled through her head, and she wondered what it would be like to have this forever. Which was about the stupidest thought she could have. Alice stiffened, pulled back.

"What's the matter now?" His voice teased.

"Uh," she faltered, her throat dry. "You were holding me so tightly." It was an idiotic thing to say.

"Didn't it feel good?"

"Yes," she whispered.

He pulled her back tightly against him again. "Then stop fighting."

Who wanted to fight? "All right." The tight, sinewy strength of his body, the firmness of his strong arms heightened the excruciating awareness of him. *Let the music never end. Let this go on forever and ever.*

Which was impossible. Even Sly Grimes's doubtful talent couldn't create something endless. "Gonna Love You Till I Die" expired painfully, and the band now launched into "Oh Susanna"…or rather, the accordion, guitar, and piano did. The snare drum had given up the ghost entirely, and the violin seemed to be struggling with a long-dead and buried "Turkey in the Straw."

Jace led Alice off the floor and disappeared into the crowd in search of refreshments. She stood there, smiling irrepressibly. She could feel the heat of his body, feel his nearness, as if they were somehow connected by an invisible elastic band.

"Well there, Alice." The familiar voice sliced into her reverie, and Alice's heart plummeted. She knew whose it was. Would recognize it anywhere. This complication was the last thing she needed. She turned with dread.

"Oh, Brad. Hello," she said with a definite lack of enthusiasm.

"Didn't know I'd find you here tonight," said Brad. He was grinning lustfully.

"Didn't know I'd find you here either," answered Alice with dismal truth.

"How's tricks?"

She winced. Perhaps she could get away, locate Jace, make some excuse so they could leave immediately, before Jace and Brad found themselves face-to-face. But the idea came too late. Jace was back by her side and handing her a frosty glass. Brad stared at him, giving him the once-over the way a cattleman would size up his competitor's bull.

"Uh, Jace, uh…" Alice began.

"Pleased to meet you, Jace." Brad thrust one hand forward. "Name's Brad."

"Pleased to meet you too, Brad," said Jace smoothly. "You must be Brad Mace, the rancher."

"That's me, all right."

"Alice was telling me about you. How are things out at Two Posts?"

"Busy, what with vaccinations and all," answered Brad, obviously pleased to have been asked about his favorite subject.

"Vaccination time, is it?"

"Yep. Gotta be careful with cattle. Gotta keep in mind the health of your herd. What you need's a good, dependable refrigerator for your vaccines and animal medications. That's not all. You know the mistake a lot of ranchers make?"

"Tell me."

"They draw up the meds with a clean needle, but then, when they get ready to vaccinate, they don't switch to another needle for the injection. Inject the animal, stick the same needle back into the bottle, and you contaminate the medication. Days later, same bottle no longer has any effect."

Ferociously, Alice chewed at her bottom lip. There

had to be a way out of this situation and out of this place.

"I'm a pretty careful guy," Brad continued. "Keep a vet box with syringes, needles, calving and breeding equipment, heat mount detectors, tattoo and ear tagging tools, thermometers, the works, and—"

"Well, there you are, the two of you. Or should I say three?" The new voice was Rose's. Rose, lovely and adorable. Rose to the rescue. If anyone could save this situation, it would be Rose. Alice could have kissed her with relief. At her side, Jonah Livingstone was still staring at her in a besotted way. Rose always did manage to do that to men.

"Brad, you're the man I want to see," exclaimed Rose. "I've a question to ask you about cattle breeds."

Rose interested in cattle breeds? Since when? Come on! Brad could see through that one, couldn't he? No, he couldn't. Rose was fluttering her eyelashes up at him, and he fell right into the honey trap.

"Fire away," said Brad, his lips spread in a blissful leer.

"I think I need a bit of air," murmured Alice, thankful for the chance to escape.

"You can have quite a lot of it, if you want," said Jace. Grinning smugly, he led her toward the back of the room, where a door was open to the cool night.

The plain stretched out in front of them, whitened by the moon's spectral light. In the distance, hills lurked, dark, mysterious, and from somewhere out on the main road came the sound of a truck changing gears. Wretched and terribly uncomfortable, she knew she would have to give Jace some sort of explanation.

"It's turned cool," Jace said to fill the silence.

"Jace, it's about Brad…"

"What about Brad?" There was a light, glancing note in his voice. Was he laughing at her dilemma? "He's everything you said he was. Tall, lean, handsome."

Alice shifted, fiddled with the sleeve of her blouse. "But he's not...well...the man in my life."

"Of course he isn't."

"What's that supposed to mean!" She was miffed at having been caught out.

"The way you look at him, for one. With bored indifference. You don't look at a lover or a fiancé in that way. And your voice—it lost that caressing, sweet note."

Alice swallowed hard. "What caressing note?"

"The note I hear when you're alone with me," he said softly.

What could she say to that? Nothing. Her own body had betrayed her; her long unused acting skills had failed her. She stared out at the desert night.

"Also, there's another thing," said Jace. "One very obvious thing."

"What?" she asked, waiting for the worst.

Jace chuckled. "Brad's a cattle rancher."

"So?"

"For heaven's sake, Alice, what do you and a cattle rancher have to talk about? You're a vegetarian. You probably don't even kill mosquitoes. Brad breeds cattle to sell for beef."

The game was up. She knew it, he knew it. "I had to invent him," she confessed.

"Why?"

"To protect myself. Against you."

Jace was silent.

If only she could read the expression on his face, Alice thought with desperation. Then she'd have a clue as to what he was thinking.

"And now?" His voice was so gentle. "Do you want to protect yourself?"

"No. I'd much rather trust you," she answered simply.

Chapter Thirteen

The Corridor

They headed home through the velvety dark. There was no wind, and far off, in the hills, the howls of coyotes filled the night. Through the corner of her eye, Alice peeked at Jace. He was off somewhere distant. Off in a world where she had no place. Was he thinking about her? Was he aware that she was there?

She searched desperately for some normal topic of conversation and didn't find one. Well, let the silence continue, she decided. And stop wondering what will happen next.

As they turned into the front yard, Jace stopped, surveyed the pile of wooden boards Pa Handy had delivered. It seemed as if a hundred years had passed since then. A hundred years and a big change in her awareness.

"I'm going to have to set aside more time to continue with my home improvement scheme," he said, his tone serious.

Her heart skipped. That meant he was going to be here for a while, didn't it? "Actually, I was thinking of buying some paint and getting started on protecting all of this before next winter comes around." Her hand waved airily at the faded building.

"You paint the house?" He sounded surprised.

She turned to him defiantly, her eyes challenging. "And why do you think I'm not capable of doing that? You may not believe this, but the inside of the house looks the way it does because of me. When I first moved back here, this was a wreck. It had been empty for years and years, and I had to plaster, paint, and pull the whole place together. Or, at least, the inside of it."

He threw up his hands in mock defeat, but his voice was placating. "Alice, I didn't really mean to doubt you."

"Yes you did," she answered stubbornly. She turned, her eyes blazing, and surveyed the house. Despite the dark, it was impossible to miss the peeling paint around the windows, the overall shabbiness. Her vexation vanished as quickly as it had come. She could see why he'd said what he had. What she didn't want to explain was that it took a certain amount of money to keep a place like this up. Money was not one of the things that slid easily into her life.

"What color?"

His question startled her out of her reflection. She blinked. Normal conversation. That was all she had to participate in. She should feel relieved. "It's always been yellow. I like the idea of a bright yellow house. And dark blue window frames." She grinned ruefully. "I suppose that's a little odd."

"Sounds nice."

"You think so?"

"I think so."

Her hand was trembling when she slid her key into the lock. Now what was going to happen? Were they going to walk up those stairs and go to their separate rooms? She didn't want that. No way. Time to put Rose's Tactic into action. How exactly could she go about doing that? He wasn't making things easy for her, not really. He had stepped in closer, was helping her out of her jacket, and her knees started knocking again. Did he have any idea what happened to her when he stood close like this?

"Jace?"

"Yes, Princess?"

Well, now what? Was she going to ask him to spend the night in her bed? Of course she wasn't. "It was nice…" She took a deep breath. "Dancing with you."

"That it was." His reply came with the barest hint of a smile. "That it was. Very nice."

She waited. Would he say something else? Make a gesture? Reach out for her?

His eyes traced the line of her mouth, caressed her face, and her skin burned as strongly as if he had touched her. But he didn't make the slightest move.

She couldn't stand here in the vestibule, waiting forever, could she? No. She couldn't. "Well, good night," she said and immediately felt like kicking herself. She'd ruined everything. But why didn't he make a move? Why had he left things up to her? Or maybe she'd been mistaken. Maybe he really didn't want her after all.

There was a strange, unreadable expression in his eyes. "Good night."

They walked up the stairs silently. Separated on the landing.

Closing her bedroom door behind her, Alice's shoulders sagged. So much for Rose and her so-called infallible Tactic.

It had been a complete failure.

****

The old wall clock chimed three. Three in the

morning? Sleep had been impossible. Now here she was, standing in the middle of the corridor, agonizing. She had lain in bed for the last two hours, tossing, turning, and agonizing. Might as well do the agonizing standing up. Still, what was she doing here in the corridor, running tonight's scenario through her head for the millionth time?

She'd failed at seducing Jace, and she didn't need Rose to tell her why. She'd stopped short of showing him how much she wanted him. But she did want him. And she was, deep inside, pretty sure he wanted her too. Although he certainly hadn't done much to show her that. Not recently, anyway. Except tonight, when they were dancing…

Your move now, Alice. What exactly would that move be? She tiptoed in the direction of Jace's door. This was ridiculous. He was probably sound asleep. He'd think she was crazy if she went in there. She tried to think of an excuse. Could she say she'd heard a noise?

A floorboard under her foot groaned. Oh God, what if he heard that? What if he came out? What would she say? "Hi, Jace. I'm standing here, lurking in the corridor and agonizing, debating whether I should go in and seduce you." Of course she couldn't say that. No way.

Jace's door swung open. There he stood, a towel tied around his waist, sarong-style. Alice's eyes traveled over the broad, wonderful expanse of his chest. His arms had the exquisite lines of a sculpture, all ropy muscle and tight tendons. He was gorgeous and utterly desirable. He must also be thinking how strange it was to find her standing out here. She was an silly fool, a total idiot. A child caught stealing cookies from a cookie jar couldn't feel guiltier.

"Alice…is something wrong? What are you doing out here in the corridor?" His face expressed concern. Surprise. And pleasure?

"Um…nothing. Nothing's wrong."

His eyes noted her pale, flimsy robe, the long curl of her hair tumbling over her shoulders, and one eyebrow quirked. "You always lurk in corridors at night?"

"I couldn't sleep." She swallowed. Oh hell! Go for it, whole hog, said her inner voice. It was a killer, that inner voice.

"And?" Casually, he leaned one shoulder against the door frame.

"Look," she swallowed again. "I was thinking of coming to your room for a visit."

"Oh?"

"You are making things difficult for me."

"What am I making difficult for you?"

"Actually, I was here, lurking in the corridor, agonizing, debating whether I should go in and seduce you."

This time the silence was long. Endless. She closed her eyes, unable to look at Jace. She hadn't really said that, had she? Oh yes, she had. Now, all that had to happen was for the mythical one-hundred-and-sixty-foot giant anaconda to slither into the corridor, open its fetid many-fanged jaw, and gobble her up. Which it didn't.

He was laughing. A sudden flood of terror and fury burned through her. She opened her eyes, glared at him. "Okay. Laugh at me." She wanted to punch him. "Talk about making a fool of myself." She made a sudden movement as if to whirl away, race back to the safety of her room, but his hand reached out, grabbed her arm and held her firmly in place.

"I'm not laughing at you." His voice had turned gritty, rough. Lifting his other hand, his fingers traced the line of her cheekbone, delicately descended to the curve of her mouth, and the hot beat of desire cannoned through her. "I'm laughing for joy. You ever heard of that?"

Joy? "Jace, I want you." It was almost a whisper. Throwing caution to the winds. "I dream about you every night."

"I can't sleep when I'm in the same house as you," he said softly. "I want you so much. I've wanted you from the first second I saw this stubborn face of yours. And your delicious, lanky body."

"Good," she said, her voice hushed, breathy. "Now we're making progress."

He stared at her. "I can hardly believe this is finally happening."

She reached out and, with the flat of her hand, followed the line of his shoulder before moving down, lacing her fingers into the curl of hair on his chest. So he could start believing.

Then, as if no words could show how deeply he wanted her, he pulled her into his arms, lowered his lips to hers, and kissed her with all the passion she could hope for. There was no resistance left in her, and her mouth softened, opened in sensual abandon. Her hands slid up, curled around his neck as she arched into him. She wanted him to feel her need, her passion. To let him know she was his tonight. She was his to love.

"I want to love you all night long," he whispered.

"All night, please," she whispered back. The heat in his eyes sent desire burning through her.

With his mouth, he traced a line of hot, sweet kisses

over her face, down her neck to the high arch of her collarbone. There was only one way she could respond. Bringing her hands down slowly over his body, she pulled him to her, cupped his firm buttocks, pulling him closer, causing him to gasp with pleasure as she undulated her hips against him.

Crushing her mouth under his, he cupped her breasts in the palms of his hands, and she moaned softly, her knees feeling as if they were giving way beneath her in the wild swirl of desire. His hardness heated her belly, telling her exactly how much he wanted her, spoke promises of the pleasure they would share, and she laughed briefly, thrilled with the power she had to excite him. Her fingers traced the line of the towel hiding his male nakedness, and she sought to undo it. Her voice was a deep sigh. "I want to see every inch of you."

"See?" The towel slid to the floor, and he was standing in front of her, hard, hot, and smooth, in all his glory.

"Touch. Lick." Her knees were about to give way. "Do you think we could get to a bed? Quickly?"

"If that's what you want," said Jace, his eyes coveting her with lascivious pleasure. "But after that, things are going to go slowly." He reached for her, his hands tracing the long line of her body. "Slowly, all night long." He nuzzled the delicate skin under her ear. "It's been hell all these weeks, knowing how close you were…so close and so far away."

"It has?"

"It has," he said simply. "I ached all over."

"All that lost time…"

He picked her up as if she weighed no more than a pinch of the desert dust, carried her to the bed.

"This has to come off." His fingers slipped under the soft fabric of her gown.

"It does," she agreed as she pulled the garment over her arms. She needed to feel his skin against hers, needed the rub of his chest against her breasts.

The silken light of the moon played over them, inviting them to taste. His hand traced her waist, her flat stomach. "Just the way I imagined it," he breathed and began exploring every inch of her. Kissing her warmth. Lingering, drawing flames, letting his tongue follow his touch, searing a hot trail over her skin and down her belly to lap the sweet dew of her femininity, never stopping, always coaxing.

She shivered against him, twisting in desire, forgetting everything but how wonderful it felt to touch him, to feel his fingers slipping deep inside her, and she exploded in sudden shuddering waves.

He lowered himself over her, and she opened to him, arching high, meeting him, enfolding him as he went deeper, brought them together. Again she moaned with searing joy. Jace, inside her. Over her. Around her. Nothing mattered but this moment. This night. All night with Jace.

Chapter Fourteen

Morning

Glaring white desert morning touched the lids of Jace's eyes. *Alice.* The name sketched itself over the surface of his mind, the way it had for some time now. This time it was different. This night had been different. Alice had lain in his arms. Incredible. He would never tire of looking at her. Of caressing those long, pale limbs, feeling the proud arch of her hips, admiring the elegance of her neck. He turned in the bed, reached for her. Her place was empty, but the warm, dusky scent of her hovered in the air.

She had been here. Unless he'd gone and invented the whole thing in his own lust-filled mind. *Impossible.* You didn't dream about making that kind of love. It had been real, all right. So, where was she now? Vanished again? Perhaps regretting the night?

Then he noticed the heavenly odor of coffee and yeasty bread drifting through the air. That was a good sign. Pulling himself out of the warm tumble of the bed, Jace hauled on a pair of jeans, made his way down to the kitchen.

Alice, her back to him, was caught in the dancing blaze of light streaming through the window and into the yellow kitchen. Her hair tumbled over her shoulders in a wild disorder. She was wearing the same thin, silken dressing gown she'd worn the night before, and the hand on her hip delineated its definite and sexy arch. His heart beat a light, staccato rhythm. Alice. *His Alice*. The thought left a soft, silvery trail in his mind. Then he pulled himself up short. *His* Alice was probably pretty wide off the mark. He braced himself for possible disappointment.

She had been his for one night of intense, heart-searing love, but she was an unknown quantity. He couldn't know what her reaction to him would be this morning. Could a woman who had shown so much passion withdraw again?

She seemed to feel his presence suddenly, although he'd made no sound, no movement. Turning, she found him there, in the doorway. Watching her. Waiting.

Shyness—that was the first expression crossing her face. Then he caught the faint, subtle bend of her body as it arched toward him, desiring him still. Saw the sweetness of her smile, caught the aura of a woman who'd spent the night loving passionately. He held his arms open, and she crossed the room with swift steps, folded herself softly against him.

"Good morning," he murmured, his mouth against hers.

"Good morning." Soft notes bespoke vulnerability.

"I was wondering if you'd run away." He was sounding pretty vulnerable, too, he knew.

She leaned back in his arms, raised her hand and traced the line of his lips with gentle fingers. "I watched you sleep. I don't know how you managed it."

"Managed what? Sleeping?"

She nodded, smiled up at him. "I…I was…I mean, the situation was too…exciting for me to want to sleep."

"We can go back to bed and try again," he said, bending down and giving her another kiss. Then, pulling back, he saw the same shyness cross her face again, followed by a faint blush.

"We could," she said softly.

"Why did you get up?"

"I..." Unsuccessfully, she tried to quash a grin. Then dissolved into embarrassed laughter. "I got hungry. And I thought that you would be hungry too, and so..."

"I'm starving. And it smells heavenly, whatever it is."

"Fresh rolls. And there are fresh coddled eggs with herbs if you want."

"Coddled eggs?"

"You'll see."

"Alice?" His tone was soft, but there was a serious note.

Her eyes questioned him, faintly wary now.

"Thank you."

"Thank you? For what?"

"For lurking in the corridor last night."

"Oh." She began laughing again.

"You'll do it again, won't you? Every night. I want you beside me every night and every morning. I want that. Very much."

Her eyes dilated with sweet pleasure; her mouth formed the words he wanted to hear. "Me too. I want that."

His heart was full, and glowing sunlight sparkled through the room danced for the two of them. "Have I told you how beautiful you are?"

Stepping away from him, she shook her head, denying his words. "You know that's not true. You don't have to say things like that."

Frowning, Jace poured out two cups of coffee and handed one to her. "I wish you wouldn't tell me what I'm supposed to think. I do think you're beautiful, or I wouldn't say it. And, by the way, absolute perfection doesn't exist."

"Of course it does. Look at you. You're beautiful…simply perfect."

"Me? Perfect?" He chuckled. "No way, Alice. Didn't you notice the bulky shape of my legs? Don't you dare look down at my feet. Talk about proportions…Michelangelo would never have used me as a model!"

"Jace, don't be silly."

"I'm not being silly. You think I'm perfect because you're in love with me."

"I'm…what?" The coffee cup clacked against the wooden table. "What did you say?"

He looked back at her calmly. "That you're in love with me."

"Not too conceited, are you? Not too sure of yourself," she spit out indignantly. "You are too much. I'm in love with you? I can't believe I'm hearing this!"

He leaned casually against the counter, perfectly pleased with himself. "Yup. You are, and you'd better start believing it, because I'm dying to hear you say those very words. I have the feeling that they'll make me feel mighty good. Let me try them out on you."

"Jace!"

"Alice Treemont, I've been in love with you for some time now."

She stared at him, her eyes wide, dark, unreadable. "Are you making fun of me? Is this your idea of a joke?"

"Then it would be a joke in very bad taste." Putting down his cup, he moved in closer, pulled her into his arms again. "Do you think you could get used to hearing that?" He nuzzled the sensitive skin at the base of her neck.

"You can't mean it." Her voice had melted like liquid honey.

"I can. Do I have to say it again right now?"

"Yes, please," she whispered.

"I love you, Alice Treemont."

She curled against him. "Okay. You win. It feels good. It feels wonderful. And I'll tell you what. I'll send the magic swinging right back in your direction. What do I have to lose? Jace Constant, I do love you."

"No kidding." He kissed her again, softly, lovingly, his mouth exploring the contour of hers. "My desert woman. As beautiful as a desert morning."

Chapter Fifteen

Moving On

Days flowed by in a haze of happiness, and the magic held. But despite the depth of their feelings, their relationship was doomed to end. Eventually. Not that Alice wanted to think about that. Not yet, anyway, even if it was like waiting for the other shoe to drop.

This evening, as she was preparing dinner, Jace walked through the door, a bottle of champagne in his hand. "Whatever you're cooking, it smells wonderful. I'm surprised that everyone in Blake's Folly isn't standing outside the front door, begging to be let in." He bent, kissed her as tenderly as always, but there was something wrong. She sensed it. Or perhaps she wasn't totally convinced by Jace's breezy manner.

"We celebrating something?" she asked lightly.

"Yup." He fetched two antique crystal glasses from a cupboard, poured out the pale golden liquid. "You're going to like this, Alice. The area around the Winterback Mine is going to become a real wildlife refuge, after all. Not a tourist site."

"Well, that certainly is wonderful news." Jace had mentioned the project several times over the last week, but she hadn't known it was so imminent.

"A place where even snakes can be free of persecution."

"At last." Their glasses clinked in a toast.

"And here's something nicer. Dr. Laura Waterton, who's in charge of the project, knows all about you. She actually reads your articles."

"She does?" Alice blinked with a mixture of pleasure and surprise. "Funny. When you sit here in Blake's Folly writing about snakes, you feel so isolated. You wonder if there really is an audience out there."

"Well, snake articles probably don't hit the best-seller list," said Jace. "But neither do history books. I doubt if a third of my friends have ever opened the ones I write. They go for the best sellers, the investigations, the glamour stories."

She looked at him curiously. "Doesn't that bother you?"

"If I let it bother me, I'd have no friends at all." He laughed shortly. "But getting back to the conservation area, Laura Waterton wanted me to ask if you were interested in getting involved out there. As their on-site herpetologist—it's a part-time position."

"Really? You're not joking?" She stared at him, hardly trusting her ears. Recognition for her work, protection for snakes? And some money in her pocket.

"Think it over, Alice. Nothing's definite yet. We're not sure that the politicians will give in to all the demands or that enough money will be allocated for the full educational project. But, if it does, at least I won't worry about you when I'm gone."

"Ah." Here it was. Her pleasure vanished. Dread and anguish slid down the length of her spine like a finger of ice. This was the beginning of a goodbye scene. When would Jace be packing his bags? Tomorrow? Any day now? In a week?

Alice put her glass down carefully on the counter. She wished she could let the subject ride, glory in the time they had left. But she couldn't. She had to know, even if the answer was painful. She tried to keep her face as expressionless as possible. "And when were you planning on leaving?"

There was a flicker in his eyes, and emotions like reserve, withdrawal, and discomfort crossed his face. Was he afraid she'd make a scene? Is that what was worrying him? Well, she had her pride. No way she'd let him know how bad this was going to be for her. She'd always known this would happen.

"I'm here for another eight days." His voice was flat. "After that, I'm expected back for a series of lectures. And there's all the publishing work to be taken care of at the university. I've been away for too long as it is."

Her mind fought to take in what her heart wanted to refuse. "Eight days?" she repeated, her voice faint. She stared down at the tabletop. Why hadn't he said anything before? The magic of the evening vanished, blown out like a candle, leaving a cold dark room behind.

"I'm afraid so."

"As in here today, gone tomorrow?" She tried to sound casual. Wasn't this what a fling was all about? What had she been hoping for? Permanence? She didn't know if she was angrier with herself or with Jace. Didn't know if it was anger she was feeling. Or frustration. Or loss.

"Alice?"

She didn't want to look up, didn't want to meet his eyes in case he read how hard this was for her. Eight days!

"Alice."

She didn't want to hear what he was going to say either. About what fun it had been. About how he hoped it had been as good for her as it had been for him. About how he'd never talked about permanence. About how she couldn't expect him to stay with her forever.

She raised her hand in the air, the palm flat, as if to stop the words. Avoid complete disaster. "No."

He resisted her plea for silence. "Alice, listen to me."

"Don't bother, Jace."

"Don't bother what?"

"Telling me we can stay friends. That you've had a lovely time. That maybe you'll come back for a visit one day because it really was so interesting."

"Is that what you want to hear?" His voice was hushed, dangerous-sounding. "Goodbye? Thanks for the fun, for the roll in the hay? It's been great, but I've got things to do, places to go, people to see. Time to get on with my life."

She raised her eyes. Finally. Looked at him. His mouth had become one grim line; his face was white. "Okay." But she braced herself for disappointment. "What did you really want to say?"

"I wanted to ask if you'd come with me."

Now she was certain she wasn't taking things in correctly. "Come with you?"

"To Chicago." She saw the hope in his face.

"Do you really mean that?"

"Of course I mean it. Will you? Come and see what my life is like?" He hesitated, as if doubting her answer. "I'd understand if you wanted to stay here, of course. I'd understand perfectly. You have new opportunities opening up, perhaps a paying job as a herpetologist out at the conservation area. I can't blame you for wanting to stay. It's…" He stopped, ran a hand through his hair, a distraught gesture. "I guess I can't see ending what we have. Not now."

Neither could she. "But how could I go to Chicago? There are the dogs…"

"I know. Come for a while, at least. We'll find someone in Blake's Folly who will take care of the dogs while you're gone. Let's see how things work out between us. See if there's a future."

Work out? She stared at him, her mind whirling. How could they possibly have a future together? Their lives were so different; there was such a distance between Nevada and Chicago. Besides, everyone knew long-distance relationships didn't work, not in the long run. And how would she fit into his city life? Did she want to? She'd already been there, done that. What if things went awfully wrong between them? What if all the magic suddenly disappeared? What if…

His eyes searched hers. He was waiting for her answer.

"Jace, what if what we feel is something that happened because you're so far from home? A bit disoriented out here in the desert. What if it doesn't stand up to life in Chicago?" She was making herself more and more miserable with every word. "What if this has been nothing more than a holiday romance?"

He shook his head, denying the possibility. "That's what we'll find out. All I know is I love you. I can't give you up. Not now." He stopped, his mouth a fine line. "But perhaps you don't feel the same way. Perhaps I'm not that important."

"Oh, Jace. You are." She threw her arms around

him. "I love you so. I'm just afraid…"

"Of what?"

She pulled back, saw the hope reflected in his every feature. He was right. What was there to fear? If they loved each other, they could make it work.

Then pursing her lips, she threw him a sly, knowing look. "Of course, there is one major problem."

"What major problem?" he said, his voice gruff.

"Tanya. How's Tanya going to like the arrangement?"

"Tanya?" Jace's face changed. He looked slightly puzzled. "What does Tanya…" He stopped.

Opening her eyes wide with pure innocence, she batted her lashes. "Perhaps we should fix Tanya up with Brad."

Chapter Sixteen

Chicago

The living room was huge. Jace's whole apartment was huge, airy, bright, and luxurious. How had he once described it? "Impersonal. An apartment. Not a home."

Well, it was impersonal. And ultra-modern. And glamorous. Not cozy. Anything but cozy. The obviously expensive furniture looked so modern, it had definitely been delivered by spaceship. On the wall hung large bright bloody-looking blobs: the contemporary abstract art Jace said he loved. Compared to her house in Blake's Folly, a place chock-full of the crumbling debris of more than a century, this apartment was, well…worse than impersonal. Secretly, Alice called it bleak. She'd been here for two weeks now and couldn't get used to the bleakness.

And what a change from Blake's Folly the center of Chicago was. A growing sense of foreboding told her she'd never adapt. Never, ever, and that would eat away at the fabric of what she and Jace shared. The surroundings were different, but Jace was still Jace. Yet with each passing day, she felt less and less like Alice.

There was nothing bleak about one room—the room Jace used as an office. There, shelves groaned under the weight of heavy tomes, some of them quite ancient. In that study, Alice felt at ease. It would be the perfect room to work in…if she'd been able to work. But where would she find a snake to study and photograph in the middle of Chicago? In the reptile zoo.

Magnificent specimens, all of them. Gleaming and passive behind the thick glass walls of their cases. Like prisoners. She was beginning to identify with their fate. Behind the wide glass windows of Jake's condominium, she was also a well-fed, very protected captive. Except she'd come here willingly. A prisoner of love.

When she was with Jace, life was glorious. He showed her the busy city, took her to concerts, to the theater, to intimate restaurants where they ate wonderful food, and in night's dark hours, their loving was sublime. But during the day, Jace was busy out at the university. That was unavoidable. He had work to catch up on, people to see. It was a temporary situation, he'd assured her. In a few weeks' time, he'd be freer. Free to spend more time with her. She knew how guilty he felt, leaving her on her own all the time. Out of her element. With no serious occupation.

Museums and art galleries were wonderful places, but not every day. What else could she do? Alice hated window-shopping. For her, sleek boutiques couldn't compare with Rose's musty shop, its treasures from another epoch, its fusty armchair where she'd sat and gossiped for hours. She tried hard not to enumerate all the other things she also missed but couldn't stop herself.

She missed her nosy, prying neighbors and wondered what they were getting up to these days; in the elevator that swooped her up to Jace's fortieth-floor apartment, people fixed their eyes on some invisible point and avoided eye contact at all costs. She missed the soft, furry presence of her dogs; pets were forbidden in this building. She missed the silent sweep of the desert, the scratch of scrub when a shivering wind curled down from the north, the sweet smell of changing seasons. She missed the moments she'd spent with Jace, tramping over that vast wasteland together.

The one thing she treasured here in Chicago was loving Jace—loving he returned fully. She'd never known such joy could exist. If only they were both in Nevada, sitting together in her yellow kitchen, exchanging the small details of a busy day. Back there, in Blake's Folly, she'd have her work, her reference books, and her photos. Perhaps a job out in the Winterback Mine Conservation Area. How frustrating to be cut loose from the life she'd created for herself in Nevada and the work she cherished.

That wasn't all. Although he never mentioned it, never even touched on the subject, Alice knew that Jace was itching to sit down, get on with the writing of his book. But he couldn't. Because she was here. If she prevented him from doing the work he loved, he'd end up feeling as frustrated as she. As far as relationships went, this was a recipe for disaster.

****

They entered the chic gallery where, tonight, there was the opening of a new exhibition. "I can finally show you off to everyone," Jace said, his voice strangely gruff as he helped her off with her coat and slid his eyes over her silky black dress. "I've been telling everyone about you, about how intelligent you are, how gorgeous. They're dying to meet you."

"They are?" A shiver of guilt flashed through her, dampening the pleasure of compliments. He wanted everyone to meet her, and she'd been dreaming of going home. Of dragging him away from his friends, his contacts, his life here. Bringing him back into hers. She felt like a spoiled, egocentric child.

"I thought everyone was here to look at art, not at me," she joked.

Jace laughed. "Yes…well…this is conceptual art, so I doubt if there will be much to see."

"Then what are we doing here?"

He shrugged. "Keeping up a presence with colleagues. Don't worry. It won't last forever."

Although, in very little time, it certainly felt as though it would.

Almost desperately, Alice tried to find either interest or meaning in a snag of tangled chicken wire in one corner: *Untitled Work* read the ticket on the wall beside it, and that was no help at all. There was a piece of tedious video art in which a man walked forward ten steps, then back, then forward again, then back. Five extremely large photos showed close-ups of a woman grimacing; this time, there was a two-page, extremely obscure explanation of the work.

Was anyone really enjoying this stuff? Alice looked around. No one seemed to be spending time looking at anything. Instead, wineglass in hand, everyone chatted— the usual cocktail conversation.

"I was right," Alice complained softly to no one in particular. "Been here, done this." Was it so different from those parties she'd once attended in Hollywood? The setting certainly wasn't similar, and the noise level was a lot lower. Maybe there were interesting conversations going on in several of the groups, but she was bored. Terribly bored, like any introvert who relished both solitude and socializing with a very few close friends. Whereas Jace, a relaxed extrovert, was chatting amiably with people he didn't know and might never see again.

A woman—was her name Lana?—turned to her. "Jace says you work with snakes?"

"Yes, that's right. I'm a herpetologist."

Lana shook a head of glossy artificially red curls and shuddered. "I'm terrified of snakes. How can you be interested in something horrible like that?"

"Do you know anything about snakes? Have you ever been close to one?" Alice kept her voice calm, cool, but she knew she was wasting her time. When would Lana ever run into a snake?

"I'd die first."

"It's an instinctive fear," said Jace, coming to the rescue. "But not something we can't get over. It takes time, effort, and curiosity about nature. I'm learning that." His eyes, warm, filled with love, met Alice's over Lana's head.

"You can't convince me," Lana insisted almost petulantly.

No. They probably couldn't.

****

"Jace."

He stood by the cocktail cabinet, pouring out two cognacs—an intimate gesture, one they shared every evening before bed.

She felt, more than saw, his body tense. As if, instinctively, he knew what she was about to say. He always sensed what she was thinking. No point in hiding anything. If she didn't use words, he seemed to pick up on her every thought telepathically. Now he raised his eyes, looked over at her, his eyes wary, his expression guarded.

"Jace. I'll have to go home soon. To Blake's Folly."
Simply said, that devastating phrase.

"Oh?" He made an effort at keeping his tone light.
"Leaving me already?"

Alice looked at him helplessly. She was destroying
the intimacy of the dark lovely night with bad news. But,
when you came down to it, was there a good time for bad
news? "This was supposed to be a short visit."

"I know. But I was hoping that a short visit meant
more than a couple of weeks." Crossing the room, he
handed her a glass, sat down beside her on the broad
leather sofa, enfolded her in the curve of his free arm. "I
know it isn't easy for you here, Alice. I wish I could get
away more, have more free time. I've been away for so
long, and there's so much catching up to do in the
publishing end of things. And with students who have
been waiting for me."

Twisting slightly, she reached up, cupped his chin in
her hand. "Don't feel guilty. It's been wonderful being
with you. I love it, and I love you."

He kissed her fingers. "But? But you're out of your
element here. That's what you want to say, isn't it?"

She forced a smile. "The weather is getting warmer,
and snakes will be coming out of their burrows. There
are photos to take, articles to write. There's a job opening
up for me."

"And you want to be back in the desert, doing all
those things."

She nodded. "Yes, I do. But we have another
problem—you know that as well as I do. Since you'll
never come out and say it, I'll say it for you." She turned
so her eyes met his squarely. "You want to get working

on your own book, don't you? But you can't. Because you feel you have to entertain me every evening when you come home. Keep me happy."

He looked slightly embarrassed, and she knew she'd guessed correctly. The time they'd spent together here in the city had also forced him to be idle. Had it been as difficult for him as for her?

He was silent for a long while. "I know how you feel," he said finally. "You're an independent woman. You're used to doing what you want when you want. I'm like that too. As I've said before, we're really very similar."

Alice nodded. "So, you see? If we go on like this, we'll ruin everything. The magic will vanish. And if it's tinged with frustration and regret, our love for each other will fade. You know it will."

"So what do you suggest we do? About us?"

"How about if we visit?" She tried to sound hopeful, make the suggestion sound viable. "You visit me in Blake's Folly; I'll visit you here in Chicago. We'll make things work out for us with no sacrifices on your part, or on mine. Goodness knows, the house in Blake's Folly is big enough for you to have your own office. Perhaps when I'm here, I can meet other herpetologists, get access to research papers." She stopped. She didn't think she could keep up the positive-sounding patter for much longer. Any minute now she might burst into tears, her heart was that heavy.

He didn't look very enthusiastic. "Maybe."

"Some people manage long-distance relationships for years on end." But not for forever, her little inner voice told her.

He leaned back, raked his fingers through his hair.

"I'd hoped for more than visits. I'd hoped that somehow we could manage to live together all the time." A rueful smile tugged his mouth. "Never having been in this position before, I suppose I thought everything was possible if I wanted it enough."

Why was he using the past tense? Didn't he think there was any hope for them anymore? Did he think everything was over? Or that she was refusing him?

"I want to be with you, too. To live with you," she said softly. It was true. She hadn't realized, until right now, how much she wanted that. To live with Jace, to wake up with him every single morning for the rest of her life, to feel his warmth beside her. Know he'd always be there, sharing. But thoughts like that belonged in never-never land. To the world of impossible things. Or to the lives other people lived. Not to her. Not with Jace.

"But you don't think it's possible." His voice was dry.

"Not like this. Not now, anyway. We'll have to find another way of doing it."

"Fine. We'll look for a solution." He sounded less sure now. As if he were giving up. Carefully he put his cognac down on the low cocktail table beside him. "So. When would you like to leave?"

She bit her lip, agonized, her heart breaking. Did he want her to go as quickly as possible now that the decision had been made? Did he want to get on with his old life now that he knew it wouldn't work with her? Because it wouldn't. Not in the long run. "In a few days," she said as calmly as she could manage.

"You set the date, and I'll make the plane reservation for you."

There was a long silence. He leaned back, closed his

eyes wearily. She knew he was hurting. She was hurting, too. But what could she do? Hope she wasn't making a terrible mistake.

He opened his eyes again, looked down at her. Some of the usual warmth and humor was back. "Alice?"

"Yes?"

"When you get home…hold off putting that 'Room to Rent' sign back up, okay?"

Chapter Seventeen

Blake's Folly

Someone turned up the terrible tinny radio, and the distorted crackle of music sounded like a bomb in Alice's ears. She bit into the chocolate chip cookie she'd been holding in her hand for the last half hour and grimaced.

Ma's cookies, so sugary they made all your teeth ache simultaneously, now tasted like musty old straw in her mouth. No, not that. Old straw would have tasted good, comparatively speaking. The coffee resembled tepid boiler fluid (although Alice didn't have much experience in the tepid boiler fluid department, she reckoned the comparison was pretty close).

All in all, she was having a miserable time at an event she normally enjoyed: Shorty Leap's annual garage sale. The garage sale was the next most important social event in Blake's Folly after the Get-Together. True, it wasn't a social event that would ever hit the Beautiful People pages of fashion magazines, but as far as old-fashioned fun went, it usually wasn't bad.

Except this year. This year it was awful. How could you have fun if you were wasting away with a broken heart?

"I hear that lodger of yours has moved on," said Mick Fletcher, her watery blue eyes full of commiseration as she swigged back her beer.

The last thing Alice wanted—or needed—was commiseration. Or pity.

"That's right," she said and tried to look as indifferent as possible. At the same moment, she was mentally kicking herself for about the thousandth time. Why hadn't she been smart enough to keep Jace as lodger material and nothing else? True, she would have missed out on a relationship of incredible emotional importance, but she would also have kept her heart intact, her life narrow and well under control. But no. She'd had to go and fall hook, line, and sinker in love. With the wrong man.

She sipped at the boiler fluid. Awful tasting, it might well be, but it was a load better than the solid core of misery turning her inside out.

"Gone back to Detroit, has he?"

"Chicago. Jace lives in Chicago, not Detroit." Hell. She didn't want to talk about him. It hurt too much. "Great coffee, huh?" But it was easier diverting a guided missile than a good, old-fashioned Blake's Folly gossip.

"Everyone figured he'd be staying on."

"Well, they figured wrong, didn't they," Alice snapped. "Perhaps everyone should have asked me outright instead of figuring."

Blatantly ignoring her comment, Mick was determined to continue. "Yep, figured he'd stick around, what with the Winterback becoming a tourist center and all that." She leaned in closer and peered into Alice's face for the coup de grâce. "I hear you're gonna do a snake show. You can make a bundle doing that. Friend of mine's uncle's cousin over at Tonopah did a thing with trained moles. Almost got on cable."

Alice shuddered at the idea of what a mole show might be. Then, a painful image of herself dressed in a spangled leotard and plastic tiara trudged through her mind. A snake show in a tourist center? This time rumor was around thirty million miles short of the truth.

"No, I'm not going to do a snake show. The Winterback Mine has been declared a conservation area. I'm setting up a snake education program and protection zone."

Mick's brow lowered with suspicion. "You ain't gonna let them things wriggle over this way?"

Alice tried not to sigh too loudly, and she reminded herself, yet again, that education begins at home. Pretty well every single resident in Blake's Folly would be bound to ask her this very same question over the next hundred years or so.

"Don't worry, Mick. We're as interested in keeping the creatures in the reserve as you are."

The project for the conservation area had panned out perfectly. The job offer had come a few weeks after her return from Chicago. Alice should have been thrilled. She'd tried to feel thrilled—but then the dead misery had come floating back in again. Look on the good side of things, she'd ordered herself. Now you'll have enough money to live on without struggling, and you'll earn that money by doing exactly what you love.

"Folks here reckoned that there lodger of yours would be staying on, the way he fixed the house up and all."

Alice plunked her cup of tepid boiler fluid down on the Formica table in front of her. Why was she drinking this awful stuff? She turned to glower at Mick. "Folks should mind their own business. Besides, Jace's work is in Chicago. He's a writer, he teaches at the university there, and he runs a publishing program. He had to go back sometime, you know. He couldn't spend his life out here gnawing spindly groat weed. And I couldn't stay in Chicago because I'm working out here. I love it here and mean to stay put. Chicago is thousands of miles away from Blake's Folly. In more ways than one."

Jace obviously meant to stay put, too. There was no more talk of permanence each time they spoke—far too occasionally for her comfort—on the phone. He missed her, he said. He loved her. She missed him too. When would they see each other again? During his summer holidays? Summer seemed like light years away.

Mick's pallid eyes were watching her steadily. "That ain't no reason."

"What ain't—isn't—any reason?" muttered Alice. She was losing the thread of the conversation.

"Distance ain't."

"Oh, but it is."

"Thought so once. But it ain't."

"What's that supposed to mean?" Alice asked testily. She didn't want to talk about this, did she? Not with Mick Fletcher of all people. Not with anyone. She hated opening her private life to public scrutiny…yet talking about things seemed to take a little hopelessness out of the situation. Mentioning Jace's name, as painful as it was, made him seem a little closer, as if he'd slipped out of the room for a moment or two.

"Thought distance made a difference, once upon a time. When I met Harry Breem back in '64. He were from down Three Stones way. Lived in a beat-up old trailer with no more cash to his name than fleas to a glass of milk. Earned about enough to keep hisself in cheap socks an' boxer shorts by catching rats."

"You...you liked him?" Alice wasn't certain she was standing on firm ground in this exchange.

"Liked him!" Mick snorted. "Fair went mad over the man. No way I was gonna live down in Three Stones, though. What with my daughter up here and all."

"What happened?" Curiosity was getting the better of her.

"Died, he did. That's what."

"Oh. I'm sorry, Mick." Alice felt embarrassed.

"Nothing to be sorry about," said Mick gruffly. "Harry was hitting ninety by then, and we'd had a good run of years together, though I sometimes wish I'd gone down there to live with him every day, like. Wouldn't have seemed so romantic that way. Not when you got pots to wash day in and day out with cold barrel water and all them dead rats lying around." She took another slug of beer.

Fighting for control, Alice looked down at the floor. She didn't want Mick to know that her stomach was aching with suppressed hilarity. "I suppose dead rats do chill the atmosphere somewhat," she finally managed to utter.

"On a daily basis, they do. Sure enough."

"Well," confided Alice, wanting to make amends for the way her mouth was twitching, "distance wasn't the main problem Jace and I were facing." She wanted to kick herself as soon as she'd said that. In another minute she'd be pouring her heart out.

Mick was scrutinizing her again. "Folks here say you was getting on fine together. Never know what really happens between two people when the lights go out and they slide in between the sheets, though."

Alice blushed deeply. "Good heavens, Mick." When people here in Blake's Folly wanted to get earthy, they went for it directly. "Things were fine when the lights went out," she answered stiffly. "But Jace is a city boy, you see. He doesn't like the desert. Not really."

"It bother him much being out here?"

Alice rolled the question around in her mind for a minute. She'd never really thought about it. "No. I don't think it did bother him. In the beginning, it did, quite a bit. But not at the end. However, it did bother me. I kept wondering if he was dreaming about being in Chicago with his friends, living the fancy life, doing the things that interest him."

"So what'd he waste time here for?" Mick grinned her smile of crooked fangs. "Things like place don't make no difference, not when you really love someone, and they love you right back. Don't get caught up on silly ideas, girl. Life ain't long enough. Besides, that man don't look like no fool to me. He needed city life and city glamour, wouldn't have started messing around with you. Wouldn't have given you a second glance, he wouldn't have."

Which made sense. Too much sense. Unless she was snatching at any illusion of hope etching itself onto her horizon. Which also meant that if there was a future for her with the man she loved—very deeply loved—then the next move was up to her. So what was she supposed to do? Give up her new job? Move to Chicago, after all? Look for a job there? Ship the dogs out to the animal shelter near Reno? All the solutions seemed so drastic.

Yet life without Jace was also hard. Every corner of her house, every inch of her bed, every square foot of the desert reminded her of him. Even out at the Winterback

Mine Conservation Area and Wildlife Refuge, people constantly asked her if she'd heard from him.

"A nice man. This project might not have gotten off the ground so quickly without his support," Pete Wilkens, the botanist, had said to her this afternoon.

A nice man, Jace? More than that. A lovely man. Did she have the guts to go back to Chicago, try and fit into his life although the situation might eventually end badly? Did she? It would be better than dreaming about him all the time, then feeling like a failure. Move to Chicago when she loved Blake's Folly? Loved the excitement of setting up the snake protection area?

Her heart felt as if it weighed a ton. There was another solution, of course. It was so big and so obvious, she'd been an utter fool not to see it: why not talk this over with Jace? Why not see what they could work out together?

"Okay," Alice said to no one in particular. "Here we go. Rats and all."

Mick Fletcher lifted her beer can in a mock salute. She didn't have the faintest idea what Alice was on about now, but it sounded good enough to her ears. "You show 'em, honey."

Chapter Eighteen

Claiming Killer

Alice got Jace's answering machine for the sixth time. He wasn't answering his cell phone either, and she didn't leave yet another message; after the first two, it would be foolish repeating herself. Where was he? Why did it always seem that when you really wanted—or needed—to talk to someone, they vanished off the surface of the Earth? Had he given up on her? Was he now sitting in some luxurious gourmet palace, talking to a dark-haired and sleek creature in designer togs?

"Of course, if you'd had the guts to stay in Chicago instead of running away, you wouldn't have to deal with a machine!" she chastised herself. And he wouldn't be out dipping steamed lobster into lemony butter sauce and eyeing the brunette over candlelight.

When she got the machine again at eleven that night, she slammed down the receiver. She had begun a serious hate relationship with telephones. After that, there was nothing she could do but toss and turn in bed for the next eight hours until it was time to get up and catch the bus that would take her out to the Winterback Mine Conservation Area.

She was locking the dogs into the kennel in the morning when she heard the telephone ringing back in the house, and she almost broke her neck in her haste to get to it.

It was Jace. Thank goodness it was Jace.

"Is everything all right?"

Damn! How she loved the deep, rich tones of his voice. "Fine," she answered breathlessly. "It's..." She was unsure about how to begin. "It's...I sort of wanted to talk to you. Sort of urgently, sort of..."

"I gathered that." His voice was dry, faintly amused.

"What do you mean?"

"You called my house seven times and the cell three."

"Oh." She was embarrassed. "How do you know that? I didn't leave more than two messages."

"Both phones told me. This is the big city, you know. It's a modern sort of place with modern conveniences that help us along in a modern world."

"Oh. Of course." Now she really did feel like a jerk. She'd never owned a cell phone, had never seen the need for one. Hadn't Jace complained about the lack of coverage in the Blake's Folly area?

"I didn't get in until two, or else I would've called earlier."

"Oh." Her repartee was more than a tad short of brilliant, she noted. What was he doing out until two in the morning? She felt a sudden stab of jealousy. Then hoped the lobster had been hard to digest. What if her proposal was going to be an unwelcome one? What if he was no longer interested? What if... *Oh, cut it out.*

She squeezed her eyes shut. "Jace, I want to see you. I think we should talk. I miss you far too much. I was silly to leave so quickly." She stopped. "Jace...more than anything, I want to be with you. Live with you all the time, not temporarily. I hate being so far away from you.

I hate this separation."

There was a long—or so it seemed to her—silence.

How idiotic she had sounded. All that gushing! She tried to be more sedate, more reasonable. "What I mean is, at least we should try. I...look, if you want, I can come back to Chicago so we can talk this over, see if there's a viable solution."

"Forget it, Alice."

"Forget what?" Her heart dropped so low so quickly, it hit the floor with a bang. Yes, she'd made a ridiculous fool of herself.

"About coming here, to Chicago."

The sudden wave of nausea was almost overpowering. This was the end. She'd lost him. It was all her fault. Her fault. Still...it hadn't taken him much time to get over her. No sleepless nights lost over Alice Treemont and the reptiles. How much was such a fickle man worth? Not much. Perhaps it was better to be rid of him after all.

"Oh." Once again, it was the best she could come up with. Then she took a deep breath. "The brunette?"

There was a second's hesitation. "What brunette?" At least he sounded genuinely puzzled.

"You know. Lobster and champagne. Et cetera."

"What lobster? What are you talking about?"

"Forget it, Jace. It's a private joke between me and Killer. So, how's tricks?"

"Alice. You were right in leaving Chicago, you know. What would you do here? I was being totally self-centered and selfish, thinking I could keep you locked up in my apartment forever, like a princess in a tower. Waiting for me to come home. It was a recipe for disaster, and you understood that better than I did."

"Well, I thought…" Her voice trailed off. Oh, why go on humiliating herself. He didn't want her there anymore, wasn't that as obvious as her two left feet?

"I've been waiting for this call, you know." There was a softness in his voice, although she couldn't interpret what it meant.

"You were?"

"I was. I was starting to think it would never come."

Meaning, she had waited too long? Meaning, now it was too late for them? She almost wept. "You really have fallen in love with someone else. Is that what you're trying to tell me?"

"Right." He sounded annoyed. "That's my style. In and out of love with someone new every half hour or so. You always this trustful?"

"Oh. Sorry." Anxiously, she glanced up at the clock. The morning bus would be passing through Blake's Folly in five minutes. "Jace, the bus. If I run, I can just about make it. I have an important meeting out at the Winterback. If I miss it, there's no way of getting out to the mine today. Unless I hitch…and if a car happens to pass this way. Look, could we talk this evening? I'll be home at around seven." Although, what in heaven's name would they talk about since there was probably no viable solution to their particular problem.

"Fine, Alice. Let's speak this evening." To her ears, he sounded as though he were about to start laughing. For the life of her, she couldn't see the humor in the conversation. Horror, yes. Humor, no. And if it were humor, why? What on earth was so funny? Or was he relieved, happy to be getting off the phone?

"And Jace?"

"Alice?"

"I love you."

"I know." He was chuckling. Damn him.

"What do you mean, you know that I love you?" Indignation was sneaking right back into the picture again. "How can you be so sure?"

"If you didn't, you wouldn't have offered to come back here to Sin City."

"Oh. Uh, and do you…" She stopped, unable to continue.

He really was laughing at her now, no mistaking that. "Yes, Alice," he said, his voice low, deep, thrilling. "Yes, I love you, too. Remember that."

****

At three minutes after seven, Alice stepped off the evening bus that had carried her back from the Winterback Mine Conservation Area and onto the dry, dusty earth of Blake's Folly. In front of her, lit by a bleak and bleaching setting sun, the main drag of this almost-forgotten semi-ghost town stretched out in all its grim glory: rusty corrugated-iron roofs, broken-down cars, trailers, shacks, clapboard horrors, dying trees, straggling dry weeds, and cracked windows. She took in the whole scruffy, bedraggled landscape and grimaced.

"You really expected Jace to love this place?" She felt like punching herself.

There was a little knot of people grouped together up near the Handy's bungalow; she could make out Ma, Pa, Jane Grimes, Mick Fletcher, and Sam Foster. All of them were standing there, watching her. Alice raised her hand in greeting. They continued to stare, silently but intently. Pa looked like he was gloating about something. She had half a mind to go over, ask what was up.

But there was no time for that; she had to get home.

Turning left at Ed Baker's shanty, she quickened her steps. Jace would be phoning soon, and the one thing she wanted at this very moment was to talk to him. Hear his voice, even if that made her seem like a silly teenager waiting for a call from a first boyfriend. She didn't, in the least, mind the comparison. Who cared? If being madly in love made you juvenile, well then, that was okay with her. Of course it would be better, a hundred, thousand, million times better, to be in his arms. But that was impossible.

Her thoughts were interrupted by the sight of a huge black animal heading full speed down the lane in her direction and leaving a swirling haze of dust and flying stones in its wake.

"Killer!" she shouted in amazement. "What in heaven's name are you doing, running free like this? You should be locked up in the kennel!"

Perhaps she hadn't closed the kennel door properly before she'd left for work this morning? Her heart sank. Damn. It was all the fault of that ringing telephone. She'd been careless, pressed for time, and hadn't bothered to go back and check.

With all his usual loving violence, Killer threw himself into her arms, liberally covered her face with kisses, as if she'd been gone for at least an ice age. Alice had to fight to keep standing. Within seconds, several other wriggling, leaping dogs surrounded her. "Oh no! You bad beasts."

What had the animals been doing all day? Making pests of themselves in the village, most likely. Riffling through people's garbage, killing chickens, trampling flowers, mauling cats, running amok. That was probably the reason everyone had been staring at her with less than the usual amiability. The whole community was probably, right at this moment, getting ready to ostracize her. Ban her from the Annual Snail Race, the Square Dance Club, and the Adopt-a-Highway Association.

"That's all I need...persona non grata in the one place I can call home." Excluded from all the Get-Togethers, Garage Sales, Old Boy's Concerts, and Bake-Ups for eternity and then some. She couldn't even run away to Chicago because Jace had said to forget it. But why? She wasn't sure she wanted to know.

The dogs trotted along beside her as she covered the last stretch of dusty trail that led in the direction of home. She climbed the little hillock where, long ago, a tent community of discouraged pioneers had temporarily settled, rounded a nasty-toothed snatch-it shrub, and started up the path.

Stopped dead.

In front of her, in the dusky light, was her yellow house with its broad veranda. In a shadow on the veranda was the tired-out rattan settee. And sitting on that settee was...

Impossible!

Jace?

Sitting there. As if that was where he belonged. There he was, all right. Looking as wonderful as she remembered, his long, muscular legs in their faded jeans stretched out in front of him, the ever-errant lock of silvering reddish hair curling over his forehead, inviting her fingers to touch.

Of course she was seeing things. She had to be. Jace couldn't really be here. Not here in Blake's Folly. Not really. Life wasn't like that. She was finally going absolutely, irrevocably mad. Having visions.

Cool green eyes watched her with amusement. Phantoms rarely looked so real.

Her courage was giving way, and she barely managed to cover the last bit of ground that led to the steps. To steady herself, she sagged against the wooden pillar of the veranda, never lifting her own eyes from that man lest he disappear like a mirage of cool, fresh water under a steaming desert sun.

He was grinning now, and in that easy, smooth way of his, the one she knew so well, he crossed one ankle over the other.

Alice stared hard, unable to say another word. Could you have conversations with ghosts?

"It's about the room," he drawled. No ghostly voice, that. It sounded real enough. A real sound from a real flesh-and-blood man. "The room you have to let."

"The room?" Slowly her brain started to function. He really was here. Yes, he was. Jace. On her settee—or was it on his settee? Because it looked to her as though that was the right place for him to be.

"Room? What room?" She desperately tried to calm the crazy hammering of her heart. "No card on the wall, mister."

"Not mister. Jace Constant. Call me Jace. Easy to remember, as far as names go."

"Impossible to forget, more like." She raised one eyebrow in an actress-y attempt to look suspicious. "I suppose you've come to claim your dog, huh?"

"Guess I have, at that. Finally. And I want to take the room too. Long term. If the snakes will have me, that is."

They were yards apart, yet the heat of him reached her, and she ached to curve into it. Into that strong, supple body of his. The warm fragrance of the man. That strange, tingling excitation she always felt in his presence began to flow through her, like sparkling, heady champagne.

"You see," he continued, "right here it feels like it might be home. The right home with the right woman. A woman with a lanky frame, golden hazel eyes, and those damned sexy, long thin lips."

"You ask my opinion," said Alice softly, "and I'd say you spell big trouble."

"Glad to hear that."

"You don't mind me asking what you're doing in these parts?" Her voice was so shaky she sounded as though she were warbling.

"Not at all. I'm a writer, you see, and interested in local history. So I reckon I'll be poking around the area for quite a long while."

"Is that so?" She nodded. She was bursting with questions, dying to know all, but she forced herself to keep her head, continue with the game. "Blake's Folly's a great place for history. Aunt Mae's Glorious White won the rat race once. That was back in '28, I think."

"Twenty-three. The twelfth of July. A hot month for sweaty work like that." He winked. "Nothing important like that gets past us researchers at the University of Nevada."

"The University of Nevada…" she began. Then stopped. Gaped. "Nevada? Why Nevada?" She couldn't be hearing right. Or he'd made a mistake…"Not Nevada…you're…"

"Nevada, all right. It was this crazy idea I had around a month ago. To offer my talent over there. My advice, my expertise in publishing. But I knew my decision all depended on something—or someone—temporarily out of my hands."

His eyes searched hers, less confidently now. As if something might go terribly wrong at the last moment. As if he were afraid that her words to him on the phone had meant less than he wanted them to. "You did say that, didn't you, Alice? About us living together permanently?"

"Oh yes! Oh yes, I said that. I meant it. Most definitely."

He grinned with relief. "Thank goodness for that. This morning, after we spoke, I called the university back. Told them I'd be flying out here to discuss the details."

"Flying?" she said vaguely. It was hard for her to take in the reality of this conversation, of this whole situation.

"Well, it's an expression we folks use up there in the big city. Technically speaking, the airplane did the flying. I simply sat in it." His green eyes mocked her.

"Oh, Jace." She sighed.

"You feel like coming over here to the settee? Talking about this at closer range?"

"I might consider doing that." Her throat was so tight she could barely squeeze out the words. She wasn't sure that her ankles and knees would support her all that distance. They didn't have to. In one swoop, he was beside her. Sweeping her into his arms. Sending her thoughts into a slow spin.

"It feels like years since I've been here," she said in a low voice.

"I know." His breath was warm in the softness of her hair. "It was hell being away from you. We're going to make this work, aren't we?"

She pulled back slightly to look into his eyes, wanting desperately to find all the answers there. "I'd like that."

"If we're willing to take a chance." His hand crept up her back under her blouse. "Or perhaps I'm strangely excited by herpetologists. A kinky sort of thing, I admit. What do you think?" His lips found the lobe of her ear and began teasing it.

"Jace!" She tried desperately to stifle the sparks of excitement that had begun coursing through her belly. "Jace, please. Wait. We have to discuss—"

"What is it you want to discuss?"

Her steady gaze met his. "You'll hate it here eventually. You know you will. No concerts, no awful art exhibitions with chicken wire sculpture, no pollution, no traffic jams. Dinner parties with Ma and Pa Handy, concerts with Sly Grimes and the Old Boy's Band. Protests against snake shows."

He touched her lips with the tips of his fingers. Silenced her. "What I want is you. You and me doing things together. Okay, maybe one day I'll want a broader horizon. Maybe...maybe not. Who knows? But if I do, we're going to work out the right way to manage it for both of us. Together." He paused, searching her face for answers. "So what do you say now?"

Wordlessly, she stared up at him, her mind buzzing. He was right. Of course he was. If he'd been willing to dream up this latest crazy scheme so it could work for the two of them, then why fight? "No objection. No argument." Not anymore.

"Good woman." He laughed quietly. "Now we can move on to things that matter." He brushed his lips over hers longingly, lingeringly. "Things like living for the moment. Damn, I've missed you so much."

"Have you?" She smiled, her eyes meltingly soft.

Like his were. Meltingly soft, sweet, and filled with love.

Jace took a deep, satisfying breath. Looked over her head, took in the broad, endless plain rolling its bumpy way to an evening sky scratched by pink. The air was pure, tangy with the scent of dust and new buds out in the scrub. Yes, everything was going to be all right.

"I guess I really have found home, after all."

A word about the author...

Writer, photographer, social critical artist, musician, and occasional actress, J. Arlene Culiner, was born in New York and raised in Toronto. She has crossed much of Europe on foot, has lived in a Hungarian mud house, a Bavarian castle, a Turkish cave-dwelling, on a Dutch canal, and in a haunted house on the English moors. She now resides in a 400-year-old former inn in a French village of no interest and, much to local dismay, protects all creatures, especially spiders and snakes. She enjoys incorporating into short stories, mysteries, narrative non-fiction, and romances her experiences in out-of-the-way communities and her conversations with strange characters. http://www.j-arleneculiner.com

Thank you for purchasing
this publication of The Wild Rose Press, Inc.

For questions or more information
contact us at
info@thewildrosepress.com.

The Wild Rose Press, Inc.
www.thewildrosepress.com